Noelle likes Noel.

Does he like her too?

Noelle's Christmas Crush
by Angela Darling

SIMON SPOTLIGHT
New York London Toronto Sydney New Delhi

SIMON SPOTLIGHT
An imprint of Simon & Schuster Children's Publishing Division
1230 Avenue of the Americas, New York, New York 10020
Copyright © 2013 by Simon & Schuster, Inc.
Text by Tracey West
Designed by Dan Potash
All rights reserved, including the right of reproduction in whole or in part in any form.
SIMON SPOTLIGHT and colophon are registered trademarks of Simon & Schuster, Inc.
For information about special discounts for bulk purchases, please contact Simon & Schuster Special Sales at 1-866-506-1949 or business@simonandschuster.com.
Manufactured in the United States of America 0813 OFF
First Edition 10 9 8 7 6 5 4 3 2 1
ISBN 978-1-4424-8337-8 (pbk)
ISBN 978-1-4424-8338-5 (hc)
ISBN 978-1-4424-8339-2 (eBook)
Library of Congress Catalog Card Number 2012956183

chapter 1

MOM IS TAKING ME BLACK FRIDAY SHOPPING.
Want 2 go? texted Jess.

Busy 2day, Noelle texted back.

Y?

U no y! *<<<<=

LOL! You are Christmas crazy.

I no. Have fun shopping!

Noelle smiled and put down the phone. Jess had been her friend since they were little, so she should have remembered that the day after Thanksgiving was a special one for Noelle. It was the official start of the Christmas season, the most important time of the year! Well, at least to Noelle. And even if it wasn't the most important time of the year, it was the best time of the year.

I guess I am Christmas crazy, Noelle thought. But she had good reason to be. Not only was she born on December 25, but her last name was Winters, and on top of all that, her parents had named her Noelle Holly. Noelle Holly Winters! She was destined to be Christmas crazy.

"Noelle, are you gonna just talk on your cell phone, or are you gonna help us?"

Noelle's teenage brother, Andrew, came in through the back door carrying a big cardboard box. She quickly slid her phone into her pocket.

"Okay! Okay! I'm helping!" Then she headed outside into the chilly late-autumn morning.

The Winters family had a shed in the backyard to hold all of their Christmas decorations. Maybe it was because of their last name or because of Noelle's special birthday, but the whole family liked to make a big deal out of Christmas.

Noelle's mom frowned when she saw her coming.

"Noelle, where is your hoodie? It's cold out here."

Noelle had thrown on some pink leggings, a pale blue T-shirt with a picture of a snowflake on it, and some ballet flats. She'd tucked her curly brown hair into a pink hair band instead of brushing it out, anxious to get the day started.

"I'm not cold," Noelle protested, but her mom stood firm.

"Hoodie. Now."

Noelle sighed and headed back into the house, just as Andrew came outside to get another box. He rolled his eyes.

"You're not even carrying anything," he grumbled.

Noelle ignored him and went to get her hoodie. Andrew had officially been a teenager for two years, and during that time she learned the best strategies for dealing with him when he got mean or rude. Ignoring him seemed to work the best.

She grabbed a hoodie and quickly went back to the shed. Noelle's dad stood on a ladder, handing down boxes and plastic bins to her mom, who stacked them by the door. Noelle spotted something silvery shining through one of the boxes.

"Ooh, I want to carry that one!" she said. "It's the Christmas angel. She's my favorite."

"Who gets excited about carrying boxes?" Andrew muttered under his breath.

Noelle forgot her rule. "Of course I'm excited. It's the first day of Christmas!"

"That makes no sense," her brother said. "There's like, only twelve days of Christmas, and Christmas is still a month away."

"But it's the first day of the Christmas season," Noelle pointed out. "It's when all the stores put up their decorations, and all the Christmas specials are on TV."

"Technically you're both right," Mrs. Winters said. "Now please stop arguing and let's get these boxes inside!"

Noelle grabbed the box with the angel in it and quickly carried it into the house. She brought the angel into the living room, where it would sit on the sill of the bay window. She opened the box and smiled at the angel's peaceful face. Noelle's grandmother had given it to the family when Noelle was born, and every year when she opened the box it was like seeing an old friend.

As she carried in more boxes, it was hard not to peek into each one. There were the ornaments: the one with the tiny handprint she had made in kindergarten;

the one shaped like a pickle, which was supposed to bring good luck; and the tiny plastic tree that opened its eyes and sang a song when someone walked by. Noelle had been scared of it as a kid, but now she thought it was funny.

"Last one," Noelle's mom said, handing her a small box.

As Noelle brought it inside, she noticed for the first time that her dad was bringing a box into the family room, a large room in the back of the house with sunny windows. She followed him inside and saw a bunch of boxes stacked up. Andrew was already taking some Christmas lights out of one of them.

"Oh, no," Noelle said. "Dad, you promised to save this room for the party!"

"What's that?" her dad asked, putting down the Santa figurine he had been holding. Mr. Winters had the same green eyes as Noelle, but his hair was red, "like Kriss Kringle," Noelle would always tease him. She gave him a different Santa every year for Christmas.

"My birthday party," Noelle repeated. "You and Mom said. This year I get to have a separate party from all the Christmas stuff, and I get to decorate this room however I want."

Mr. Winters scratched his head. "I think we did say that, didn't we."

"Say what?" Noelle's mom asked as she entered the room.

"That I could have my birthday party in here this year, with no Christmas decorations, just birthday decorations," Noelle repeated.

"Oh yes, yes you're right," Mrs. Winters said. "Let's move these boxes into the living room, then. I'm sure we'll find a place for these decorations somewhere else. If not, they can go back in the shed."

"Well, *I'm* not carrying them back out there," Andrew said loudly.

"Come on, let's get these boxes into the living room," Mr. Winters said cheerfully.

Andrew looked right at Noelle and rolled his eyes. "Why do you have to make such a big deal about your birthday?" he asked.

"Because even though it's awesome having a birthday on Christmas, it can also be *not* awesome," Noelle replied. "Some people are so busy with Christmas that they forget my birthday. And all the decorations that are up are red and green and white, and my favorite colors are pink and purple."

Those were just some of the reasons. Peppermint and gumdrops were nice, but by the time her birthday came around she was a little sick of them; she wanted a regular birthday cake, not a gingerbread one. And there was something about celebrating her birthday and Christmas on the same day that made each thing feel just a tiny bit less special.

"Mom, can we get the party decorations today?" Noelle asked.

Mrs. Winters shook her head. "The stores will be crazy today, hon. And we're getting the tree. We're going to concentrate on Christmas first. But soon, I promise. It's a little early to be decorating for the party, anyway."

Noelle looked around the family room. "I have some awesome ideas," she said. "Lots of balloons. And streamers. And in the flyer for the party store I saw this whole decoration kit with pink and purple flowered plates and stuff. I want everything to be perfect!"

Her mom sighed. "It will be lovely. But remember nothing is ever perfect, honey."

"If you try hard enough it can be," Noelle insisted. "And I plan on making this the perfect party."

Mr. Winters stuck his head through the door. "What

do you say we get that tree? I want to get there before the good ones are gone. And we need some place to put all these ornaments!"

Noelle laughed. "We'll probably be the first ones anywhere to get our tree," she said, but she was excited. Once the tree was up, it would feel like Christmas for real. And that would mean her birthday was getting close too.

The family bundled into the car and drove to the fire station in downtown Pine Valley. They always got their tree from the parking lot next door, because some of the profits went to the firehouse. Mrs. Winters popped a Christmas music CD into the dashboard.

"Might as well get into the spirit," she said.

It seemed to work, because Andrew and Noelle didn't argue at all on the drive (which only took ten minutes), and when they pulled up into the lot with all the trees stacked up by the metal fence, Noelle felt a big surge of Christmas spirit.

A car pulled out past them, with a Christmas tree tied to the roof.

"I knew it! They got the best one!" Mr. Winters joked.

"I guess we're too late then, Scott," Mrs. Winters teased.

"They didn't look hard enough," Noelle said. "We'll find the best one."

They climbed out of the car and searched the lot. Mrs. Winters stood back and watched; she knew her family well. Noelle and Andrew would each quickly find a tree that they were certain was "the best," but Mr. Winters would examine just about every single tree in the place until he found the perfect one.

And that's exactly what happened. Right away, Noelle found a tree with a round, fluffy shape, and Andrew went to the tallest tree in the lot.

"Dad! Dad! Over here!" they yelled.

But Mr. Winters methodically went through the lot, stopping to touch the needles of a tree, or standing back from it and looking at it with squinted eyes. Everyone waited impatiently until he finally called out, "I've got it!"

They circled around the tree he had propped up. It was tall, but not as tall as the tree Andrew had picked. It was round and fluffy, but not as wide as Noelle's tree. It was the very best of both. Everyone had to agree that it was perfect.

"You've done it again," Noelle's mom said, grabbing his arm and kissing him on the cheek.

By the time the tree was tied to the roof, everyone was hungry, so they stopped at the drive-through and ordered a sack of burgers and four peppermint milkshakes, a special treat for tree-trimming day.

They spent the rest of the afternoon putting up decorations and hanging ornaments on the tree. Noelle carefully went through the box and picked out her favorites to hang, and Andrew did the same. It was kind of an unspoken agreement between them. Andrew got to hang the little wooden train and the pinecone ornament that he made in second grade, and Noelle got to put up her handprint and the little birds in nests that clipped onto the branches. The only one they ever argued about was the pickle.

This time, they reached into the ornament box for the pickle at the same time. They both stopped, and then Andrew shrugged.

"Go ahead," Andrew said.

Looks like someone has found the Christmas spirit after all! Noelle wanted to say, but she knew better. She just smiled and hung the pickle on the tree, right in the middle.

Mrs. Winters stood in the middle of the room with her

hands on her hips and looked around.

"Everything looks beautiful," she said.

Noelle looked around. A garland of green branches and berries was draped across the fireplace, and her dad's Santa collection adorned the mantel. The tree was lit with dozens of tiny white lights, and a big glowing star shined at the top. Mr. Winters had hung white lights in the window, and their glow illuminated the silvery angel standing beneath them.

"It's perfect," Noelle agreed. "See Mom? Some things can be perfect."

Her mom smiled and shook her head. "Well, it *will* be perfect once we get all these storage boxes put away."

Mr. Winters sank into the armchair next to the tree. "Can we do it later? I was thinking of heating up the leftover turkey for some sandwiches for dinner."

"Yeah, we've been doing stuff all day," Andrew added.

"Fine, then," Mrs. Winters said. "Let's take a break. I'll call you when dinner's ready."

"I can work on my party planning!" Noelle announced, and then she ran up to her room.

Last year she had received a laptop for her birthday, and it was the perfect gift—not just because it was pink.

She had started right away planning the party for this year. She'd saved pictures of party decorations and cakes, and made lists of what she would need. She had also bookmarked a free site where she could make awesome e-mail invitations to send out to her friends.

She sat on her bed and turned on the laptop, going right to the invitation site. She had a tentative guest list working, but she hadn't hit send yet. She stared at one name on the list: Noel Shepherd.

Just hit send, she told herself. *What's the worst that could happen?*

But she chickened out, just as she had yesterday and the day before that.

Maybe tomorrow, she thought, and then she clicked over to the birthday recipe site.

chapter 2

"SO I STILL CAN'T DECIDE BETWEEN PARTY decorations that are pink and purple or just picking one color and sticking to it," Noelle said at lunch on Monday.

She sat at a round table with her three best friends, Jess, Alyson, and Hailey. All three girls had known each other since elementary school, which had made going to middle school a lot easier, Noelle thought. She knew a lot of girls who had stopped being friends once they got into seventh grade, but luckily that hadn't happened with them.

"I don't know about pink," Alyson said thoughtfully, twirling a lock of blond hair around her index finger. "If everything is all pink, it could look like a baby shower or something, you know?"

Noelle nodded. "I know. But it's hard to choose just one color. I like them both the same."

"Pick pink!" Hailey suggested. "It's the least Christmasy

one, and you're kind of doing an anti-Christmas thing, right?"

"Well, not *anti*-Christmas, exactly," Noelle corrected her. "I mean, I still love Christmas. But I really want to keep my birthday separate."

"I think you are birthday obsessed now," Jess teased. "We'd better change the subject or else I won't be able to think of anything besides birthdays all day."

"Can we talk about tofu turkey, then?" Hailey asked, holding up her sandwich. "As in, if I have to eat any more of this tofu turkey, I'm going to turn into one?"

The friends laughed.

"Mom slipped a turkey sandwich into my lunch bag without telling me," Jess said.

"My dad did this," Alyson said, holding up a fancy-looking little morsel. "He rolled up the turkey with some lettuce and cream cheese in a tortilla, and then cut it into little rounds. He calls it 'turkey sushi'."

Hailey got a dreamy look in her eyes. "Mmm, sushi. Mom used to pack me her Korean vegetable sushi almost every day. Just last week I told her I was getting a little tired of it. I think she's punishing me with tofu turkey."

Noelle swallowed a bite of the turkey sandwich her dad had packed for her. "I don't know, I kind of like all the turkey leftovers."

"That's because they make you think of Christmas," Jess pointed out. "And you, Noelle, are Christmas crazy, I told you."

"You said I was birthday party crazy," Noelle reminded her.

Jess shook her head. "Both. How will we put up with you all month?"

"She's allowed to be party crazy," Alyson said. "My Bat Mitzvah is in April, and I'm already planning it. This weekend I found the perfect dress online."

Noelle sighed. "A dress! I haven't even thought about what I should wear. I guess I should match the decorations, right?"

"Can I come dressed as an elf?" Hailey asked.

Noelle laughed. Hailey was always saying random things like that.

"Why do you want to come dressed as an elf?" she asked.

"Well, I got this awesome elf costume at the mall, and I can wear it on Christmas and Christmas Eve, but that's only two days," Hailey said. "So your party would be one more day I could wear it."

"Well, I guess you can wear whatever you want," Noelle replied. "But I was kind of hoping there would be no Christmas stuff at this party, you know?"

"Whoa, harsh!" Jess said. "Noelle, you are becoming like one of those girls on that *Sixteen and Spoiled* show. Except you're not turning sixteen."

"Hardly," said Noelle, then she started to giggle. "Remember when that girl had a fit because she wanted an elephant at her party, and her parents wouldn't let her? Can you imagine?"

"I don't think you could fit an elephant in your living room," Hailey commented.

"Ooh, you could be like that girl who made all of her friends wear the same color to her party," Alyson said, excited. "You could make everyone wear pink."

"Ew!" Jess said. She hated pink; her favorite color was blue, and she wore a blue hair band in her auburn hair every day.

She turned to Noelle. "No offense."

"No, I know, that's too severe," Noelle said. "Everyone can wear whatever they want. Even elf costumes, I guess."

"You are too nice, Noelle," Alyson said.

Hailey nodded. "That comes from being born on Christmas," she added. "But I can leave my elf costume at home. It's no big deal."

"Thanks," Noelle said. "Now I just need to figure out what I'm going to wear."

"Can I help you pick something out?" Alyson asked. "I have become a sort of fashion expert after the search for my Bat Mitzvah dress."

"Definitely!" Noelle said gratefully.

Then the loudspeaker in the cafeteria beeped, and everyone got quiet, waiting to hear the announcement that was coming.

"Hi, everyone," said a boy's voice. "This is just a reminder that we need volunteers to help out at the Student Council's clothing and food drive on Saturday. If you can help out, please come to the gym at nine a.m. on Saturday morning. Thanks!"

Noelle must have been blushing, because Jess said, "Oh wait, that was *Noel*, wasn't it?"

"Yes, it was Noel," Noelle replied, trying to sound like it was no big deal. "Who else would be nice enough to make an announcement about the clothing and food drive?"

"He *is* supernice," Hailey agreed.

"Soooooooo nice," Alyson added.

"It's kind of weird," Jess chimed in. "I mean, he's like, perfect. He's president of the Student Council, he's on the soccer team, and he volunteers for all kinds of stuff."

"You forgot the most important thing," Noelle said.

"What's that?" Jess asked.

"He was born on Christmas Eve!" Noelle reminded her. "That's why his parents named him Noel." *And why we are perfect for each other,* she added to herself, and then she blushed at the thought.

"Well, I like that he's always smiling," Hailey said. "Like you, Noelle. And he's always nice to me, even on that day in science when I accidentally set my textbook on fire and everyone was making fun of me."

"You're right," Noelle said. "That is the best thing about him."

Then she saw Noel walk into the lunchroom. He had brown hair that sometimes got in his eyes, which were dark pools of chocolate brown. He was as cute as he was nice. Anyone else that cute and popular would have been stuck up, but Noel never acted that way.

"You know, I think I'm going to volunteer on

Saturday," Noelle announced to her friends.

Jess grinned. "I bet I know the reason why. And it begins with *N*."

"And rhymes with 'coal,'" Hailey added.

Noelle blushed. "The reason I'm doing it is that helping people is the right thing to do during the holidays," she said. "And since I was born on Christmas, I need to do all that holiday goodwill stuff. It's in my blood."

"We should all help!" Hailey suggested. "We could all use some good karma. I know I do after that brussels sprouts incident."

"Hey, speak for yourself!" Jess said in mock offense.

"No, she's right," Alyson said. "It doesn't hurt to have some extra good karma lying around."

"Fine then," Noelle said. "We'll do it for good karma."

Then she cast another glance at Noel. He was laughing at something, and his whole face just seemed to light up when he smiled.

And the fact that Noel will be there is just a bonus, she thought.

Jess stared at Hailey. "What exactly is the brussels sprouts incident, anyway?"

Hailey shook her head. "You don't want to know.

Let's just say that my little brother had nightmares for a week, and it was all my fault."

The girls laughed.

"Now let's all eat our delicious turkey," Noelle joked, and everyone cracked up again.

"NOELLE, DID YOU SEND OUT YOUR BIRTHDAY party invitations yet?" her mom asked that night at dinner.

Noelle looked down at her plate of mac and cheese. "Um, not yet," she replied. She hoped her mom didn't ask why, because it would be too embarrassing to explain. *Well, it's because I'm not sure if I should invite Noel Shepherd or not, because if he says no, I'll be supersad, and that's just weird and silly because I barely know him, right?*

"Well, please do it tonight," Mrs. Winters said. "The party is in a few weeks, and people need to make sure the day is free on their calendars. Plus we'll need to know how many people to expect so we can plan."

"Everybody in the world already knows about her party," Andrew said. "It's all she talks about."

"It's not *all* I talk about," Noelle protested, but then she added, "Well, mostly, I guess."

"After dinner," Mrs. Winters said, "okay?"

Noelle nodded and gulped.

So a short while later Noelle was on the invitation site on the laptop upstairs in her bedroom. She clicked on the guest list, but she still didn't know what to do.

She quickly texted Jess.

Sending out my party invites. Not sure if I should invite NS.

NS? Jess texted back.

Noel.

Why not?

What if he says no? Rejection stinks.

Who cares? Party will be awesome anyway because

I will be there.

Noelle smiled. LOL! She texted. Thx, Jess!

Feeling more confident, Noelle clicked on "Add Guest" and started to type.

N-o-e . . .

Then she stopped. She didn't know his e-mail address! All of the other kids she knew were in her directory from elementary school, but Noel had gone to the school on the other side of town.

It's a sign, she thought. *It's not meant to be.*

"Noelle, have you sent out those invitations yet?" her mom called upstairs.

"Just doing it now!" Noelle yelled back. With a sigh, she hit the "Send Invites" button.

At least I'll see him on Saturday, she thought.

Knowing she would see Noel on Saturday was on her mind all week. When Saturday morning came, she woke up to the sound of a text from Jess.

Mom's picking u up at 8:45.

K, Noelle texted back.

She climbed out of bed and grabbed a pair of jeans that was half hanging from one of her drawers and started to get dressed. There was a tap on her door.

"I'm changing," Noelle called.

"Okay, just wanted to make sure you were up. Mom's making eggnog pancakes," her dad answered through the door. "She wants you to eat before Mrs. Rubio picks you up."

"Okay!" Noelle replied, and her stomach started to rumble. Her mom's eggnog pancakes were delicious, and they always put her in a Christmas mood. She opened a dresser drawer that was crammed with Christmas-themed shirts. People loved to give her Christmas shirts as presents, and it was starting to get a little out of hand. But today she was in the holiday spirit.

She flipped through the pile of shirts. Santa? Sparkly tree on a black background? Cute reindeer? Stylish flying reindeer? Snowman? Ho-Ho-Ho?

She finally decided on the sparkly tree and slipped it on. After all, it was a *holiday* food and clothing drive, and Noelle was kind of a pro at spreading holiday cheer. She brushed her hair and smoothed it down. She wished Mom would let her start wearing lip gloss. Oh well, it would probably come off when she ate breakfast anyway.

Then she bounded downstairs and wolfed down her eggnog pancakes. They were moist and fluffy and tasted like eggnog with a hint of nutmeg.

"These are perfect!" she happily told her mom. "Thanks!"

"Noelle, it's a nice thing you're doing this morning," Mrs. Winters told her. "I didn't want you volunteering on an empty stomach."

Then a car horn beeped outside, and Noelle rushed up from the table.

"Gotta go!"

"Brush your teeth first!" Mrs. Winters said. "I'll tell Jess's mom to wait, and I'll bring out that bag of food we're donating."

A few minutes later, Noelle slipped into the backseat of the Rubios' car, joining Hailey and Alyson. Jess turned around from her place in the front seat.

"Is your breath minty fresh?" Jess teased.

Noelle smiled, showing her teeth. "Yes, and my teeth are pearly white. Sorry I was late. Mom made eggnog pancakes."

"That sounds awesome!" Hailey said beside her.

Mrs. Rubio nodded from the front seat. "I'll have to ask your mom for the recipe."

She drove off, and the girls reached the school a few minutes later. Jess's mom popped open the hatch in the back and the girls loaded up with bags of food and clothes for the drive.

They were right on time, but the gym was already buzzing with activity. Mr. Clark, the Student Council advisor, was frantically trying to organize the bags of clothes and food that were coming in, while a bunch of kids milled about, looking confused mostly. Noelle quickly spotted Noel sorting through a pile of clothes on a folding table.

Her friends saw her looking.

"Noelle and Noel, Noelle and Noel," sang Alyson and Hailey to the tune of the Christmas song, and then they burst out giggling.

Noelle blushed. "Yeah, he's here. So what?"

"You invited him to your party, right?" Jess asked.

"Not yet," Noelle said. "I don't have his e-mail address."

"You have to invite him," Hailey said, wiggling her eyebrows. "Then maybe you could get him under the mistletoe."

Her friends burst out giggling again, and Noelle thought she might melt into the floor from embarrassment. Luckily, Mr. Clark saved her.

"Okay, all student volunteers, circle up!" he yelled

over the din. He had a loud voice, and everyone moved quickly about, surrounding him.

He looked down at a clipboard. "All right, we need a team of kids at the entrance, helping people get bags out of their cars." He pointed to four kids. "You, you, you, and you."

Then he glanced at Noel. "You're sorting clothes, right? Let's get you a partner at your table."

Then he pointed right at Noelle!

"Noel and Noelle, you're a team," he said, and then he smiled when he realized how that sounded. "Noel and Noelle . . . that's perfect together!"

Noelle desperately tried not to blush, but she felt her cheeks grow hot. Behind her, she could hear her friends giggling. She was dying to look at Noel, to see his expression, but she didn't dare.

Mr. Clark assigned the rest of the tasks and then clapped his hands.

"All right, everybody, let's make this work!" he shouted, and everyone ran to do their job.

Noelle followed Noel to the table where he'd been working.

"Hi, there," he said with a smile. "Okay, so basically,

we need to sort out the clothes into four piles: men, women, boys, and girls. And we should try to fold everything."

"Like laundry day," Noelle said, and Noel smiled. "No problem."

"I like your shirt," he said. "I love this time of year, don't you?"

He picked up a T-shirt and started folding it, and Noelle got up the courage to reply.

"Yeah, sure," she said, and then she scolded herself. *C'mon, Noelle. You have a better answer than that.* "I mean, I really love this time of year. It's my birthday, too. And I was named Noelle after Christmas. Because my birthday is around Christmas. On Christmas. I mean, I was born on Christmas Day. You were born on Christmas Eve, right?"

She was so nervous that she could barely stammer out her reply.

That was so not graceful. Or cool. Or smooth. Pull yourself together!

She picked up a sweater and started folding it.

"Yeah," Noel replied. "I was a Christmas Eve baby. My mom keeps telling me that Christmas babies are special. So I guess you're special too."

Folding the clothes had a relaxing effect on Noelle. Plus, Noel was so nice. *Okay,* she thought. *You can do this. Just be normal.*

"It's pretty fun to have a Christmas birthday," Noelle said, talking more normally this time. "Everyone is always in such a good mood."

"I know!" Noel said. "And everyone thinks Christmas birthdays are so cool."

"Except when they forget about them," Noelle pointed out.

Noel smiled knowingly. "What about when they do the 'two for one' gift?"

Noelle nodded. "Exactly!" she cried. And then before she could even think about it, she found herself saying, "And for the past few years my birthday party has been combined with our family Christmas party. Which is okay but kind of stinks, too. So this year I am totally having a separate birthday party before Christmas. So it's separate. It's going to be great. You should totally come."

Oh *no!* Did she just invite him to her birthday party in the uncoolest way, like, ever?

Yes, you did! Noelle fretted. She wanted to climb

under the folding table and hide there.

But Noel gave her a friendly smile. "That sounds great. I'd love to. I love parties. Especially at Christmas time."

Noelle couldn't quite believe it. He was coming! But she didn't even tell him when it was. Should she tell him? And of course he didn't even know where she lived . . .

She took a breath. "Can I have your e-mail so I can send you an invitation?" she asked.

Noel whipped out a small notebook and pen from his back pocket and wrote his e-mail address on it.

"Thanks," Noelle said as he handed it to her. She tucked it into her pocket, trying to act casual, like someone who got e-mail addresses from boys every day.

The rest of the morning flew by as bag after bag of clothes was delivered to their table to be folded. They talked some more about school and people they knew, but mostly they sorted and folded as quickly as they could. Well, Noelle started to slow down a little on purpose when they were almost done. She could have folded clothes with Noel forever. She kept touching her pocket to make sure the note with his e-mail address was still there.

Finally, every last piece of clothing was in its proper place.

"Good work, people!" Mr. Clark said in his loud voice. "You guys are amazing. If your ride is here, you can head outside."

Jess, Alyson, and Hailey ran up to the table.

"My dad is here to pick us up," Alyson said.

Rats, thought Noelle. Alyson's dad was always early for everything. She wished Hailey's mom was picking them up today. She was always late.

Noelle turned and waved good-bye to Noel, and he waved back.

"Bye, Christmas-birthday buddy!" he said.

She smiled. "Bye!"

Her friends started to giggle behind her, and Noelle turned and quickly pulled them toward the door.

"Oh my gosh, that was so cute!" Hailey said, and Noelle didn't argue.

Noel was definitely cute. And he said he would come to her party!

AS SOON AS ALYSON'S DAD DROPPED NOELLE OFF, she ran upstairs to her room and flipped open her laptop.

"Noelle? Is that you? How did everything go?" her mom called up the stairs.

"Fine," Noelle called back, not taking her eyes off the screen. She went right to the invitation website and clicked on "Add Guest." She typed in Noel's e-mail address, and then, closing her eyes, she made a little wish as she hit send.

Please let him say yes!

She stood up and walked away from the laptop. Then she counted to ten out loud.

"One-one thousand, two-one thousand . . ."

Right after she hit "ten-one thousand," she clicked on "Check Replies." She scrolled through the "yes," list and saw Jess, Alyson, and Hailey, of course, and her grandma, and Madeline, her friend from chorus. But no Noel. Not yet.

Well, what did you think? she scolded herself. *It's only been ten seconds! He might not even be home yet.*

Mrs. Winters walked into the room. "Lunch will be ready in a minute. What kind of homework do you have this weekend?"

"I have to study for a math test," Noelle reported, "and my world civ poster is due. Jess is going to come over tomorrow to work on it with me, if that's okay. After her basketball practice."

"That's fine," her mom said. Then she got a mischievous smile on her face. "The Holiday Channel is starting their Christmas movie marathon tonight at seven. I'm thinking cocoa, popcorn, slippers . . . what do you say?"

"What do you think I'm going to say?" Noelle replied with a grin. "Of course!"

Christmas movies were another reason why Noelle loved Christmas so much. Even the bad movies had lots of snow and lights and decorations, and they all had a happy ending.

That night after dinner, Noelle took her favorite space on the comfy green couch (last cushion on the right). Her mom made cocoa, and her dad made popcorn. Then they watched two movies in a row. The first was a corny one about a Christmas choir trying to win a contest, but it had the snow and the lights and the decorations and the happy endings, so that was all good. Andrew stepped into the living room and rolled his eyes when he saw that one. But the second one was a comedy, *Elf*, and Andrew came in to watch it, even though he was texting most of the time.

"Bedtime, Noelle," her mom said with a yawn when the movie ended, and Noelle didn't argue. First she checked her e-mail: no new responses. Noelle sighed. Well, maybe he just didn't have a chance to respond yet. Or maybe he had to ask his parents. She decided not to worry about it. After all, he said he would be glad to come. "Just think happy thoughts," she said, which is what her mom told her to do when she was worrying too much and couldn't fall asleep. She dozed off dreaming of Christmas carols and cocoa and feeling extra-Christmasy. It was a nice feeling.

The next day Jess came over in the afternoon, wearing her green Pine Valley Basketball T-shirt (PV HOOPS) and sweats. Her auburn hair was pulled back in a ponytail, as usual.

"How was practice?" Noelle asked as they headed into the family room.

"Good," Jess replied. "I wish you were playing."

"I'm too short," Noelle protested.

"You are not," Jess said. "You're taller than half the girls on my team."

"Well, it's too fast," Noelle said.

"It's not faster than soccer, and you're great at soccer," Jess pointed out. "You should play."

Noelle had known Jess a long time—since second grade, when Jess was new in school and Mrs. Keystone had assigned Noelle to be her buddy. She knew a lot about her friend, including the fact that Jess was impossible to argue with.

"I'm not playing basketball," Noelle said flatly. "It takes place in the winter, and I'm busy in the winter with . . . winter stuff. But I'm joining track in the spring, I promise."

"Fine," Jess said. She looked around the family room. "Wait, something's wrong in here. There's no Christmas stuff."

"Didn't I tell you?" Noelle asked. "Mom says I get the whole room just for my party this year. It's a Christmas-free birthday zone."

Jess nodded. "Cool. I can't wait for your party. Hey, did you ever invite Noel?"

"Last night," Noelle answered. "He gave me his e-mail address at the thing yesterday. But he hasn't replied yet. I checked, like, ten times this morning."

"Well, it hasn't even been twenty-four hours," Jess reasoned. "He probably has to ask if he can go, and you know what that's like. It's hard to get a straight answer from parents sometimes."

Noelle nodded. That's what she had been thinking too, but hearing Jess say it made her feel better.

The family room had a table and chairs by the window on the back wall. Jess plopped her backpack on the table.

"You have the poster board, right?" she asked. "I brought markers. And we might need to print stuff out."

"No problem," Noelle said. "I'll get what we need."

A few minutes later the girls sat down to work on their posters.

"So it's supposed to be a travel poster for ancient Babylon," Noelle said. She had her hands on her hips and was staring at the blank page. "Let's see . . . there's the Hanging Gardens, and the Ishtar Gate, and the Euphrates River . . . I think you're right. We should probably print out some pictures of this stuff. It's not so easy to draw."

She started searching for images on her laptop. "We can print out whatever we want. The printer's in my mom's office."

The girls sent a bunch of images to the printer, and Noelle went to get them. On the way back, her cell phone buzzed in her pocket. She opened it to find a dozen photos from Alyson.

"What are you looking at?" Jess asked, taking the printed pages from her.

"Alyson is sending me pictures of dresses for my party," Noelle said, sliding into her chair. "Some of them are so beautiful! Check out this pink one."

She held out the photo in front of Jess's face.

"I don't know," Jess said. "It looks kind of spring-like, you know?"

Noelle scrolled through the photos. She stopped at a deep purple, shimmery dress and showed it to Jess.

"The sleeves are kind of puffy," Jess said, "and the color reminds me of grape juice. But it's nice, I guess. So, do you want this picture of the gardens for your poster?"

Noelle took the picture from Jess without taking her eyes off the phone. If Jess sounded annoyed, Noelle didn't notice.

"Oh my gosh! This one is perfect. It's not a grapey purple at all. What color would you call this?" she asked, showing Jess the phone again.

"I don't know. Ask Alyson," Jess said as she cut out a picture for her poster.

"Good idea," Noelle said. She started typing.

What color is this?

Violet, Alyson replied. Isn't it gr8?

Luv it! Noelle replied. But it's like, $300!???!!

Don't worry. It's a hot color this year. We can find one like it in the mall for a lot cheaper.

Will you shop with me?

Of course! ☺ Alyson texted back.

Thank you! BBFN.

TTYL!

"This is great," Noelle said, looking around the family room. "I think I finally know the color scheme for my party. I'll use violet, with maybe a little pink thrown in. That would look awesome, and I can combine it with silver or black even."

"That does sound nice." Jess said. She held up the poster she was working on. "What do you think? Are the letters big enough?"

But Noelle had wandered off to the lamp next to the couch. "Maybe we could find a violet lightbulb, and then the whole room would glow purple!" she said excitedly. "Wouldn't that be amazing?"

Jess put down her poster. "It sounds amazing. But are we going to work on our posters, or are you going birthday crazy again?"

"What? Oh yeah, sure," Noelle said, hurrying back to the table. "Sorry."

She picked out a few of the pictures they had printed out, and then she went over to the laptop.

"Are you printing out something else?" Jess asked.

"I just want to check the invitation site again," Noelle said, "to see if Noel replied."

Jess shook her head. "You are seriously deranged.

CRUSH

You need to chill out about Noel. And this whole party thing. It's just a party."

"It's not *just* a party," Noelle insisted. "It's my first non-Christmas birthday-only party."

Jess held up her hands. "Okay, I get it," she said. "But you should still chill out about Noel. Give him some time to reply. In fact, I dare you not to look at your replies for a whole day."

Noelle looked stricken. "You mean not until tomorrow afternoon? That's impossible."

"It wouldn't be a challenge if it wasn't hard," Jess pointed out. "How about until tomorrow morning then?"

Noelle sighed. "All right, I'll try."

"Good," Jess said. "Hey, I know you're, like, anti-Christmas and pro-birthday this year or whatever, but I started making your present. It's going to be awesome."

"I'm not anti-Christmas, I swear," Noelle said. "And um, that's cool. I can't wait to see it."

The girls had been exchanging gifts since the first year they met, but they had one rule: the gift had to be handmade. Last year Jess had made Noelle a pair of earrings with little pink stones, and Noelle had created a gingerbread basketball court for Jess, complete with

gingerbread players. But this year Noelle hadn't even thought of an idea yet. Her mind was too filled up with birthday party plans (and to be honest, a little bit of Noel as well).

"I can't wait to see mine either," Jess said.

Noelle quickly changed the subject. "Hey, I think your letters are the perfect size," she said, and the girls got back to work on their posters.

Noelle tried to keep from checking her invitation replies even when Jess wasn't watching her. She didn't check them after dinner, or after her shower, or even before bed.

But she couldn't go to sleep. She gave herself about five minutes, and then she got out of bed and turned on her laptop in the dark.

1 New Reply.

Feeling hopeful, she clicked . . . and saw it was from her aunt Jane. With a sigh, she closed her laptop.

Jess was right. She needed to chill out about Noel. But that wasn't going to be easy.

chapter 5

HEY, DID YOU GET MY INVITATION?

Did you get my invite?

Did you get that e-mail about my party?

Noelle didn't even open her laptop the next morning. But what if she ran into Noel in school? She'd have to say something about the party, right?

On the bus ride to school, Noelle practiced what she would say if she ran into him. She didn't usually get to see him, because they didn't have any classes together except lunch. Noel was almost never at lunch, because the student council and some of the other groups he was in met during lunch, and when he was there, he was always surrounded by all of his guy friends. Noelle and the other girls usually steered clear of the boys' lunch tables; they were way too rowdy.

But she might bump into him in the hallway. You

never knew, so it was good to be prepared.

"So how'd you do?" Jess asked when she got on the bus and slid into the seat next to Noelle.

Noelle knew what she meant. "I didn't check it," Noelle replied. But she avoided her friend's eyes.

"You checked it!" Jess said accusingly. "I knew you would."

Noelle sighed. "I couldn't sleep. But I haven't checked it since last night, I swear."

Jess shook her head. "You are hopeless."

Noelle felt bad about giving in, but she felt worse about the fact that Noel hadn't responded. Maybe Jess sensed this, because she put her arm around Noelle. "It's going to be an amazing party whether he comes or not," she said. "And I still think he's going to come. Just wait."

"Oh, I hope so," said Noelle. She already felt so much better.

"You are still pretty hopeless, though," said Jess as the bus reached the next stop, and Hailey and Alyson got on.

"What's hopeless?" Hailey asked.

"Nothing," Noelle answered firmly, casting a warning look at Jess. "Alyson, thanks for sending me those pictures last night. I've decided to do a whole violet theme for my party."

"When are we going dress shopping?" Alyson asked.

"I have to ask my mom," Noelle replied. "I think we're getting the party decorations tonight. I can't wait!"

"A violet dress? That sounds pretty," Hailey remarked.

"I'm so glad we're talking about this party again," Jess mumbled, but Noelle didn't hear her.

The bus pulled up to Pine Valley School. The girls got off the bus and walked through the wide front entrance into the main hallway. The bus usually arrived ten minutes before the first bell, which gave them time to get to their lockers, talk, and check out the school notice board.

"Hey, the Holiday Craft Bazaar is Thursday," Hailey said, pointing.

Jess nodded. "I made a bunch of bracelets for it."

"Like those ones you made last year? They sold out fast," Alyson said.

Once again Noelle remembered that she would have to think of an idea for Jess's present soon. Then she noticed something on the board.

"Oh, they're looking for volunteers," she said, reading a flyer with the title Holiday Heroes Program. "They match up a middle school student with a student with special needs to help them pick out presents at the craft bazaar. That sounds really nice."

She looked at the sign-up sheet, and saw a name that made her stomach do a little flip: Noel Shepherd. Of course it was like him to do something so nice!

Noelle searched her backpack for a pen. "I'm going to sign up."

Jess stepped up to the list and raised an eyebrow. "Aha! It's because Noel signed up, right?"

"No, it's because it's a nice thing to do," Noelle protested, which was true. It was also true that seeing Noel's name on the list was an extra incentive. "I can't help it if I've got extra Christmas cheer to spread around. What's wrong with Christmas cheer?"

"Yeah, what's wrong with Christmas cheer?" Hailey repeated.

"Or Hanukkah cheer?" Alyson added.

"Nothing," Jess said. "It's just—oh, never mind."

Noelle signed her name on the list. "Good. Let's get to class."

As Noelle suspected, she didn't get a chance to talk to Noel about the party that day. He wasn't at lunch, and she didn't run into him in the hallway.

After school she headed up to her room to get her homework done. She turned on her laptop so she could log on to the math practice site her teacher had set up.

The invitation site popped up on her screen—she hadn't checked it last night.

"Might as well look," she said. "It's been almost a whole day."

1 New Reply.

Noelle took a deep breath and clicked. There, under the "yes" column, was a new name: Noel Shepherd.

Noelle let out a happy cheer, then quickly realized what she was doing and became quiet. She didn't want her parents or Andrew to ask why she was doing a happy dance. So she logged on to the math site with a big smile on her face. Noel was coming to her party!

As she studied, she started to sing. *"Deck the halls with boughs of holly . . ."* She couldn't help it. She felt like she had more Christmas cheer than ever!

chapter 6

AFTER DINNER THAT NIGHT NOELLE SWITCHED back into birthday mode.

"I finished my homework," she said to her mom. "Can we go to the party store? Please?"

"Well, if you're sure you're finished, I don't see why not," Mrs. Winters replied. "No tests tomorrow?"

Noelle shook her head. "Nope."

"Hey, how come *I* can't shop for decorations?" Mr. Winters asked in a mock-hurt voice.

"You can come if you want, Dad," Noelle said, "but it's not Christmas decorations. It's birthday decorations. In violet."

"I like violet," her dad said. "But this sounds like a two-person job. I'll do the dishes."

"I've got homework," Andrew said quickly, making it clear that he was not available for any kind of dish washing.

Noelle ran and grabbed her coat. "I cut out the coupons from this weekend's flyer so we can get some good deals." She picked up a binder from the counter. "See? It's all organized in here."

Mrs. Winters shook her head. "That's wonderful. Maybe you could carry that organization over to your bedroom, too."

Noelle made a face. "Very funny. Come on, let's go!"

Party World was located just a short drive away, over on the highway. Noelle loved going there any time of year. When they pulled up, a giant inflatable Santa stood by the front entrance, waving at customers. Red and green floodlights bathed the whole storefront so that it could be seen from far away.

Noelle grabbed a shopping cart, and they stepped inside. The first display they saw contained dozens of sparkling silver snowflakes. Mrs. Winters walked up and touched one.

"These are so pretty!" she exclaimed. "Wouldn't they look nice on the back porch?"

Noelle grabbed her mother by the sleeve. "We are *not* here to look at Christmas decorations. We are here to get birthday supplies. Come on!"

Mrs. Winters gave a funny little pout as Noelle led her down the first aisle past racks and racks of Christmas items. They turned the corner and wound up in the birthday aisle, which was smooshed in the back of the store during the month of December.

Noelle opened her binder. "Okay, so we need to get some things from a few different places. The Mardi Gras section has purple streamers that are pretty close to violet. The Floral Collection has these small silver vases, and we can get violet flowers to put in them. In Sweet Sixteen they have those cool crepe paper balls that you can hang from the ceiling, in silver, pink, and violet. I'm still not sure about the plates, cups, and napkins, but I have a few choices that we can check out."

"I have never seen you so focused," Mrs. Winters said, shaking her head again. "But I'm impressed. Lead the way!"

They found the streamers first, and then the crepe paper balls. Noelle was starting to get excited. Everything looked so much cooler in person than it did in the flyer or in the pictures she had seen online.

Then they found the vases, which were cube-shaped and only four inches high. "I think we should get six,"

Noelle said, holding one up. "We can line them up along the food table."

Mrs. Winters raised an eyebrow. "You said you have a coupon, right?"

"Thirty percent off the entire purchase," Noelle reported.

"Okay then," Mrs. Winters said, and Noelle happily put the vases in her cart.

"Now we need the flowers," Noelle said. "They are the perfect shade of violet; I couldn't believe it when I saw them online."

By the time they got to checkout, the cart was filled with everything Noelle had hoped for. She looked in the cart, pleased. "Flowers, decorations, napkins, plates, knives, forks, cups, favor bags, tablecloth . . . I think that's everything."

"It better be," Mrs. Winters said with a teasing grin.

When they got home, Noelle piled every bag in her arms, carried them to the family room, and threw off her coat. Then she started opening the bags.

"Noelle, what are you doing?" her mom asked.

"I'm putting up the decorations," Noelle replied.

Her mom looked at the clock. "Your bedtime's in an

hour, and you still need to shower." Then she laughed. "Hey, I just rhymed! But I'm serious. This is no time to decorate."

"Please?" Noelle begged. "Can I just get it started? I'll do it all myself. And I'll stop in a half hour and shower. See? I can rhyme too."

Mrs. Winters sighed. "Thirty minutes, and no more," she said, leaving the family room.

Noelle looked around the room. She could set up the table first, she thought, but then she noticed that it was strewn with video game discs and open game covers. She marched over to the stairs.

"Andrew!" she yelled.

"What? I'm in the kitchen!" Andrew yelled back, annoyed.

She headed to the kitchen, where her brother was doing homework on the kitchen table.

"Andrew, you need to clean up your video games from yesterday," she said crossly. "I need to decorate for my party."

"Your party's not for like, two weeks," Andrew said. "Besides, I'm doing homework."

"But I only have a half an hour to set up!" she wailed. "It's not fair. Come on, please?"

Andrew rolled his eyes. "Whatever you say, Sergeant Birthday."

He got up and started to walk to the family room.

"What does that mean?" Noelle asked.

"It means you are bossing everyone around about your stupid birthday," he said.

He scooped up the games, brought them over to the storage cube where they were kept, and dumped them in. Then he slammed the lid shut.

"Happy, Sergeant Birthday?" he asked.

"Yes. Thank you," Noelle said stubbornly.

Andrew stomped out of the family room, and Noelle began to unpack the bags of party supplies.

Sergeant Birthday. Was she really that bossy? Her friends had teased her about being like those girls on that TV show. But those girls were horrible.

Noelle kept looking at the clock as she frantically tried to set up the tablecloth and the silver vases. She would never finish tonight, but she wanted to get as much done as she could.

It seemed like no time at all before her mom came into the room and said, "Okay, Noelle, time to shower."

"Please can I just finish the table?" Noelle asked.

"We had a deal," Mrs. Winters said. "You can do more tomorrow night when your homework's done. This is not the party to end all parties, Noelle. You need to relax and enjoy yourself a little."

Noelle sighed. "Okay," she said, reluctantly putting down the flowers she was holding.

Her mom just didn't understand. This was her first real, separate birthday ever. And on top of that, Noel was coming.

How was she supposed to relax?

ON TUESDAY AND WEDNESDAY, NOELLE MADE SURE
to do her homework right after school so that she could
decorate for the birthday party when she was done.

"Almost perfect," she said, examining the room
on Wednesday night. Hanging the pink, silver, and
violet crepe paper balls hadn't been easy, but her dad
had helped. They hung from the ceiling at different
heights, making the room look really festive. The table
was set with a violet tablecloth and the row of violet
flowers in their silver vases. She had tried putting up
the violet streamers in a bunch of different ways, but
had settled for hanging them over the windows and
the doorway.

She still hadn't found the violet lightbulbs she had
dreamed of, but she had some ideas for that. Still, even
without them, the room looked pretty good.

Andrew walked into the room and made a face.

"I can't even bring my friends in here now," he said. "It's like purple and pink threw up all over. Thanks."

"Well, I wouldn't want them in here anyway," Noelle shot back. "They'll mess everything up."

Andrew ignored her and left, and Noelle looked at the clock. She had just enough time to set out her outfit for tomorrow. The Holiday Heroes event was after school, and she knew it might be the only time all week she would be in the same room as Noel.

She stared at her closet, wondering what to wear. The days were getting colder now, so a sweater would work. Since it was Holiday Heroes, something with holiday flair might be nice. Just like with T-shirts, she had been given a lot of sweaters as gifts, and some from last year still fit.

She opened her sweater drawer and started rifling through them. Nothing green or red—that would be too much. Then she found a white one with a silver bell on the front. Perfect! She could wear her denim skirt and white leggings and her blue boots with the fuzz around the top.

Satisfied, she changed into pajamas and fell asleep, feeling excited about the next day.

When she woke up the next morning, she quickly got dressed. She checked out her look in the mirror, and she noticed a stain on the bottom of the white sweater that she hadn't seen before. Taking a closer look, she realized it was hot chocolate.

"Oh no," she sighed. She ran to the bathroom and splashed some water on it, but the stain didn't go away, it just got wider and blotchier. Frustrated, she stomped back to her room and threw off the sweater.

What now? She grabbed the first sweater she saw, a red one with a green wreath on it, and put it on. Looking in the mirror, she frowned. It didn't go with the white leggings or blue boots at all.

Back to the sweater drawer. She pulled out a dark blue sweater with silver stars on it, but when she tried it on, the sleeves were too short.

"Oh, come on!" she complained. She went back to the drawer and frantically started pulling sweaters out of it, scattering them across the floor. But nothing else looked like it would work. Everything was green or red.

"Noelle, please come down for breakfast!" her mom called upstairs.

"Coming!" Noelle yelled back.

She stared at the pile of sweaters, wanting to cry. Taking a deep breath, she opened her T-shirt drawer.

"Gotta have something blue and white in here," she mumbled, and then she found it—a light blue long-sleeved shirt with some pink flowers embroidered around the collar. It wasn't Christmasy, but it went with the rest of her outfit.

She put it on and looked in the mirror. "Per—" she began, but stopped. Her hair was a mess! It was thick and curly, and Noelle didn't mind when it got a little unruly sometimes. But all of that sweater-changing had made it look like a tangled bird's nest.

"Noelle!" her mom called up again.

"Just a minute!" Noelle yelled.

She went back to the bathroom and squirted some anti-frizz lotion into her hands and then ran it through her hair. That usually calmed it down. She ran back to her room and combed it through, and now it looked weirdly flat.

Headband, she thought. That should work. She kept them on a hook hanging next to her dresser, but the pile

CRUSH

was all tangled. She had to unravel a bunch of them until she got to the white one she wanted.

She couldn't resist one last look in the mirror. She sighed with relief.

"Perfect!" she said, and then she ran downstairs.

Her mom was standing by the open front door, looking down the street, where the bus stopped for the middle school kids in the neighborhood.

"The bus just left," Mrs. Winters reported, in that flat voice she used when she was trying not to get upset. "Go grab a muffin or something. I'll drive you."

Noelle felt terrible. She knew that now her mom would have to rush to get to work, and this wasn't how she wanted to start her day. Luckily, Mrs. Winters didn't seem to be too upset, especially after turning on the Christmas music station while they drove to school. "I think it's wonderful that you're doing so much volunteering this season, sweetie," she said. "I'm proud of you for really getting into the holiday spirit."

"Thanks, Mom," said Noelle, and kissed her mom good-bye. She felt bad about making her late, and a little guilty that some of her volunteering was motivated by Noel. "I'm sorry about running late. I'll try harder tomorrow."

"Thank you, sweetheart," said Mom. "Have a good day. I love you!"

Noelle found her friends in the front hall.

"Hey, we thought you were sick!" Hailey said.

"Just late," Noelle explained.

"You look nice," Alyson remarked.

Jess wiggled her eyebrows. "Yeah, I bet I know why. You're volunteering today, right?"

Noelle blushed. "Can't I look nice for no reason?"

"You mean *Noel* reason," Hailey joked, and Jess and Alyson burst into giggles.

"Ha-ha," Noelle said dryly, but she knew her friends were right. If Noel wasn't doing Holiday Heroes, she probably would have just worn jeans and a goofy Santa shirt. She suddenly felt silly.

Is this what happens when you like someone? she wondered. *You start acting all crazy?*

Then the morning bell rang, and the girls all dispersed to their classes. Noelle's stomach was fluttery all day, but not just because she was going to see Noel. She hadn't really thought much about what it meant to volunteer for Holiday Heroes until today. What exactly did she have to do?

During homeroom, she looked over the instruction sheet she had received. The kids from the special-needs classes would be attending the fair after school, and a volunteer would be paired with each kid. Each volunteer should help their buddy find the holiday presents they needed. Sounded pretty straightforward.

But Noelle wasn't sure what to expect. What if her buddy didn't like her? This year she had a girl in her world civ class, Chloe, who had Down syndrome. Noelle had never really talked to her, but Chloe was friends with a girl named Andrea, and they always sat together. They talked and laughed just like Noelle and her friends did. Chloe was quieter than most kids in the class, but she raised her hand and answered questions and stuff. She was pretty much a normal kid.

Maybe I'll get someone like Chloe, Noelle hoped. *That won't be too hard.*

When the last bell of the day rang, she still felt a little nervous. She quickly adjusted her headband in her locker mirror and then ran to the school's multi-purpose room.

The large square room had a high ceiling and windows on one wall that let in the fading afternoon sunlight. Rows of folding tables contained dozens of crafts handmade by students and parents. The proceeds all went to help the school.

Three moms were setting up cash boxes at a table on the far wall, and Mr. Clark was there again, getting ready to organize the volunteers. Noelle saw Noel across the room, but he was busy talking to some other kids and didn't see her. She started to move toward him, when Mr. Clark started to shout out instructions.

"Okay, here's how it's going to work!" he barked. "I need you guys to form a line at the entrance to the room. Mrs. Delgado is going to bring the kids in, and you guys can pair up with them one by one as they come in. So please put on a name tag and line up!"

Everyone obeyed quickly, but as they lined up at the door, Noelle found that she couldn't get near Noel at all. Then Mrs. Delgado appeared in the doorway, wearing a red sweater with a snowman on it.

"What a lovely group of volunteers," she said. "Now, listen to what your buddy is shopping for and try to help him or her find the perfect present. There's a big selection this year. Let's start pairing you up."

Noelle waited impatiently for her turn as she watched

Noel get paired with a boy and then head off toward the tables. Finally, she reached the front of the line.

"Hello, Noelle," Mrs. Delgado said, looking down at her name tag. "This is Eliza."

Eliza had short brown hair and wide brown eyes, and she stared at Noelle a little nervously.

"Hi, Eliza," Noelle said, in that high voice she reserved for her little cousins.

Eliza didn't say anything.

"Come on, let's go shop," Noelle said brightly. "I love to shop, don't you?"

Eliza still didn't reply, but she followed Noelle away from the line.

"Who are you getting a present for?" Noelle asked, and to her relief, Eliza answered her this time.

"Mom," she said.

Noelle nodded. "Okay. Let's go look at some stuff."

She scanned the room and saw Noel at a table with knitted scarves and hats, so she steered Eliza that way.

"How about a hat?" Noelle asked. She picked up a blue hat with a pom-pom on top just as Noel and the boy he was with headed to another table.

Eliza just looked at Noelle.

"Okay, a scarf, maybe?" Noelle suggested, but Eliza shook her head.

"No, she has a scarf!"

Noelle glanced around again and saw Noel over by a table with some soaps and candles, so she led Eliza there.

"Ooh, look Eliza, those are pretty," Noelle said, still in her high voice. She picked up a bar of soap and held it out under Eliza's nose.

Eliza made a face. "Gross!"

Noelle sighed and turned to see if Noel was still there, but he and the boy had moved on. She spotted him over by the jewelry table.

"Maybe she'd like some jewelry," Noelle said, starting to feel frustrated.

"Why do we keep walking near that boy?" Eliza asked, in the loudest voice she had used all day. Noelle flushed, hoping that Noel didn't hear. He was just a few feet away, but he didn't look up at her.

"What do you mean? We must just be shopping for the same things," Noelle said, trying to sound casual.

"I don't want to get jewelry," Eliza insisted, pouting.

"We can at least look," Noelle said. She stepped up

to the table, right across from Noel, who looked up and smiled at her.

"Oh, hi, Noel," she said. "I didn't know you were doing this too!"

"Yes, we did see him!" Eliza insisted, and Noelle felt like melting into the floor. Noel just gave her an awkward smile.

"This is James," he said. "He's looking for some jewelry for his sister, but I don't know what to do. Can you help?"

"How old is your sister?" Noelle asked James.

"She's thirteen," James replied.

"I bet she'd love a bracelet," Noelle said. "My friend Jess made some really beautiful ones."

She moved down the table toward the bracelets, and James followed her on the other side. Behind her, she heard Eliza, who sounded upset.

"My mom doesn't like bracelets!" she said loudly.

Noelle started to panic a little bit. She felt bad. She had been so worried about seeing Noel that she hadn't been very helpful to Eliza.

Noel scooted around the table.

"Hey, I'm Noel," he said, talking in his normal,

soft, friendly voice. "Are you looking for a present for your mom?"

Eliza nodded.

"My mom really likes to cook. Does yours?" Noel asked.

"She loves to cook," Eliza replied.

"There's a table over there with some cool cooking stuff," Noel said. "I'll show you while Noelle helps James."

Eliza followed Noel, and Noelle was grateful—and impressed. Noel didn't talk to Eliza like she was six or different or anything. He was just his nice, sweet self.

Noelle turned to James. "Let's pick out a really pretty bracelet for your sister, okay?" she said.

She picked up one made of red and silver beads. "Does your sister like red?"

James shook his head. "No. Purple is her favorite color."

Noelle spotted a purple beaded bracelet in the group and picked it up. "What about this one?"

James smiled. "That's nice."

Noelle smiled back. "Great. Let's go pay for it."

Noelle took James over to the checkout station and helped him pay for the gift. She glanced behind them and saw Noel with Eliza, who was holding a handmade bowl and smiling happily.

Noelle waved, and she and James walked over. "We found a really pretty bracelet that I think James's sister is going to love. I know *I* would."

James smiled broadly.

"Look!" said Eliza. "Noel found the best present ever for my mom!"

"That is really nice," said Noelle. "I bet she'll love it."

"Thanks for helping James," said Noel.

"Thanks for helping Eliza," said Noelle.

"You worked as a good team," said Eliza.

"We did!" said Noel.

Noelle felt herself blush.

"Your face is getting pink!" said Eliza.

Noelle felt herself turn from pink to red. "It's a little hot in here," said Noelle. Then she and Noel helped Eliza and James find their parents, who were waiting to pick them up.

"Bye!" she waved to Noel as she practically ran to Dad's car.

"Bye, Noelle!" called Eliza. "Merry Christmas!"

Lying in bed that night Noelle couldn't help thinking about everything that happened that day—and everything that she had learned. For one thing, picking out the perfect outfit on a school morning just wasn't worth it. It wasn't that important, and it wasn't fair to Mom to make her late.

And then there was what she had learned from Noel. To just be nice, and to be yourself, no matter who you were with. It was a good thing to remember.

And of course, it made her ♥ him even more.

chapter 8

SATURDAY MORNING NOELLE WAS STILL IN HER
pajamas, searching the Internet on her laptop. She really
wanted to find those lightbulbs for her party, and time was
running out.

As she was searching, she noticed some new e-mails
in her inbox and decided to check them out. The first one
was from her grandmother.

> Hi, sweetie.
>
> Did you get the e-mail I sent you last week? We
> need to schedule our cookie-baking day soon.
> Christmas is getting close—and so is your party!
>
> Love,
> Grandma Ruth

Noelle felt a pang of guilt. She scrolled through her messages and found an e-mail from her grandmother that had been sent days ago; Noelle had been too busy searching for party supplies to answer it. Every year she and Grandma Ruth got together and baked batches of holiday cookies. They froze some for Christmas Day, and packaged others to give out as gifts. Noelle loved doing it; it was a special day between her and her grandmother, and she always had fun. (And the cookies were delicious, besides!)

> Sorry Grandma! I've been really busy with the birthday party.

Noelle paused, thinking of her schedule. Next weekend was her party, so it would have to be this weekend. She was planning on making Jess's present tomorrow, but that would have to wait.

> How about tomorrow? Noelle typed, and then she hit send.

The e-mail from her grandmother reminded Noelle of all of the other things she had forgotten to do. She had bought her mother some candles at the craft fair, but she still had to find a present for her brother and her dad. Then she'd have to wrap everything. And make cards for her friends.

She glanced at the corner of her room, where the box of decorations marked NOELLE'S ROOM sat. Every year she decorated her room for Christmas. Andrew had already done his, and it looked awesome—a crazy mess of blinking Christmas lights. But the only things decorating her room were some stray socks and the sweaters that she still hadn't put back in her drawer.

Noelle shut the laptop, jumped out of bed, and quickly got dressed. If she didn't act fast, she'd never get anything done!

First she cleaned up her room. She put laundry in the little pink hamper and folded the sweaters, returning them to the drawers. She made her bed, then straightened the papers on her desk and the books on the pink bookshelf next to it.

Next Noelle carefully unpacked the contents of the box and set them on her bedspread. She hung the white icicle lights above her window, stringing them on the permanent hooks her dad installed to make decorating easier. Then she stuck the snowflake-shaped lights to the window itself, using the suction cups attached to them.

Then she took the items on top of her dresser and placed them in the now-empty box. She replaced them with the collection of Christmas-themed snow globes; her dad gave her a new one every year. Grandma Ruth always gave her an angel figurine on her birthday, and she added those to the display as well. She plugged in the lights and then stood back to admire her work.

Then she heard a knock on the door.

"Come in!"

"Hey, sweetie," her dad said. "Your grandma just called and said you two were going to decorate cookies tomorrow. I'll bring you over early."

Suddenly he noticed the Christmas decorations. "Hey, I thought it was only birthday and no Christmas this year?"

"It was never going to be *no* Christmas," Noelle said. "Just Christmas with more birthday balance, that's all."

"In that case, we should get the tree for your room," Mr. Winters said, grinning.

Ever since her first birthday, her father had bought a

small real tree for her bedroom. They decorated it with a popcorn garland and homemade ornaments that Noelle had made. Noelle couldn't believe she had forgotten about it this year.

"Can we go now?" she asked.

"Sure," her dad replied. "I'll meet you downstairs. But dress warmly. We had a cold snap last night."

Noelle opened her newly straightened sweater drawer and carefully removed a red sweater with a green Christmas tree on it. Then she put on her blue boots and headed down the stairs.

They drove back to the tree place next to the firehouse, which was a lot emptier than it was on the day after Thanksgiving.

"Maybe they don't have any more little trees," Noelle said, worried.

"They always have the perfect one," Mr. Winters assured her. "Just wait."

Her father was right. Noelle spotted the tree as soon as she got out of the car. It was about three feet tall and leaning all by itself against one side of the fence. Noelle ran up to it.

"It's perfect!"

"Yes, it is," Mr. Winters said with a nod. "Let me get the tree guy."

Soon they were back at the house.

"I'll get the tree stand from the shed," her dad said. "I think the ornaments are there too. Why don't you start on the popcorn?"

"Okay!" Noelle replied happily. She ran inside, threw off her coat, and popped a bag of plain popcorn in the microwave. Then she ran upstairs to dig her sewing kit out of her closet so she could string the popcorn. She found it easily, and located a needle and spool of white thread among a mess of material scraps, felt, and buttons.

I should make something for Jess out of this stuff, she thought, but then the smell of popcorn hit her nose and she headed back downstairs. In the kitchen, Andrew was opening the bag and was about to stick his hand in.

"Stop!" Noelle yelled. "That's for my tree."

"Aw, come on. It smells so good," Andrew said.

Noelle opened the cabinet and took out another bag of popcorn. She marched up to him, took the popped bag out of his hands, and gave him the new bag.

"There," she said firmly. Then she poured the

popcorn into a bowl and brought it upstairs.

She sat on her bed, threaded a sewing needle with a long piece of thread, and used the needle to string one piece of popcorn on the thread. Making a long garland could take a while, but Noelle always liked the process. It was kind of relaxing.

While she worked, her dad set up the Christmas tree stand and then inserted the tree. It fit perfectly right underneath her window.

"How's the popcorn coming?" he asked.

Noelle held up the strand, which now reached the floor. "Pretty good."

"I'll put some little white lights on the tree, and then we can add the garland, and then the ornaments," her dad said.

Mrs. Winters came into the room, carrying a box wrapped in pink-and-purple paper.

"I've got an early birthday present for you," she said, smiling.

"Really?" Noelle asked, excited. She put the popcorn garland aside and took the package from her mom. She carefully lifted up the tape, not wanting to tear the paper. "It's so pretty, and it matches the party. Maybe I can make something out of it."

When the paper was neatly folded and put aside, Noelle lifted the box lid. Inside was a beautiful violet blanket with tiny rows of pink knitted throughout.

"This is perfect!" Noelle said, holding it up. "Did you knit this?"

Her mom nodded. "I was going to wait until your birthday to give it to you, but it matches your party, and it's so cold out today, I thought you might need it."

"I love it!" Noelle cried, tossing the blanket aside to jump up and hug her mom. "Thank you!"

"I'm going to make some cocoa," Mrs. Winters said. "It's that kind of day."

An hour later the popcorn garland was strung on the tree, and Noelle and her dad were hanging the last of the homemade ornaments. Then her father pulled the gold clip-on star from the box and handed it to her.

"Put it on and make a wish," he said.

Noelle clipped the star to the top and closed her eyes. The wish quickly came into her mind.

I wish Noel likes me, she thought.

"Was it a good wish?" her dad asked when she opened her eyes.

Noelle smiled. "Really good."

That night Noelle snuggled into her bed underneath her new blanket. She had turned off the bright lights in the window but left on the lights of the Christmas tree, which cast a soft, gentle glow around the room. She breathed in the scent of pine.

Christmas and her birthday were only two weeks away! And her party was in a week! She could hardly wait for either one.

I wonder if Noel has a tree in his room too, Noelle thought. Did his family make a big deal about Christmas? Did he have a collection of Christmas sweaters just like she did? She had seen him wear a tree shirt that one time, so maybe he did. Maybe they were stuffed in a drawer, just like hers.

She wondered if he was thinking of her, too. She looked up at the star on her tiny tree and smiled.

If her wish came true, this would be the best birthday and Christmas ever.

"IS THAT MY CHRISTMAS ANGEL?" GRANDMA RUTH
asked, giving Noelle a big hug.

"Hi, Grandma," Noelle said, her face buried in her grandmother's red apron. Grandma Ruth always smelled like peppermint no matter what time of year it was.

Grandma Ruth released her and then stood back, looking her over. "Look how beautiful you are! I can't believe you're going to be another year older!"

"I can," Noelle said.

"What time should I pick her up, Mom?" Mr. Winters asked.

"When I call you," Grandma Ruth replied. "We've got a lot of cookies to bake."

Noelle's dad leaned down and kissed his mother. Grandma Ruth looked like she was about two feet shorter than he was. Noelle sometimes wondered how they could be mother and son, but she had seen pictures of her grandmother with her father's red hair, before it had turned white.

"Now scoot," Grandma Ruth told Mr. Winters. "Noelle and I need to get busy."

Noelle hung up her coat on the coat rack and followed her grandmother into the tiny kitchen. Grandma Ruth's house was small, which was perfect for just her, but Noelle's dad and his two sisters had grown up there. Noelle had no idea how they all fit.

Grandma Ruth had organized the small kitchen for cookie baking with military precision. Green mixing bowls were neatly stacked on the table; cookie sheets lined with parchment paper were stacked on the stovetop; the counter held Grandma's metal containers of flour and sugar, next to a neat line of measuring cups. Her grandmother had also set out a big bottle of vanilla, a canister of baking powder, and a jar of cinnamon—all essential for making Christmas cookies.

Next to the bowls on the table was the dented old recipe box, which contained hundreds of recipes written in Grandma's pretty handwriting on stained index cards.

"What are we making first?" Noelle asked.

"Let's make the sugar cookie dough, and while it's chilling, we can work on the peanut butter cookies," Grandma suggested.

"Okay," Noelle said. "Should I start measuring out the flour and stuff?"

"Please do," Grandma said. "I've got some butter softening on the windowsill. I'll start creaming it with the sugar."

Noelle carefully scooped the flour into the measuring cup, and then smoothed over the top with the back of a butter knife to make sure it was level. As she worked, she thought about the first time she had helped, when she was just three. She didn't remember much; her grandmother had let her stir some things with a spoon and dump some already-measured flour into the bowl.

Andrew used to bake cookies too, and Noelle remembered being jealous when he was allowed to break the eggs and Grandma Ruth said she was too little. The first time she cracked an egg into the bowl, she had thought it was the biggest thrill ever.

A couple of years ago Andrew decided he didn't want to bake cookies anymore.

"That's fine," Grandma Ruth had said. "Cookie baking

is not for everyone. And Noelle is the best assistant I could ask for." Noelle had never felt prouder.

And last year Grandma Ruth had started to let her do more things on her own. She'd handed her the recipe card for the butterscotch cookies and said, "Why don't you start the batter for this one?" And Noelle had known just what to do.

"I'm ready for the flour," Grandma Ruth said, rousing Noelle from her thoughts.

Noelle slowly poured the flour into the bowl as her grandmother mixed it in with a hand beater.

"Jess's mom has one of those stand mixers," Noelle reported. "It's pretty cool. You just press a button and the machine does the work."

"My beater works just fine," her grandmother said, giving it a final turn around the bowl. "See? And now I use the best tool of all—my hands."

She reached into the bowl and squeezed the dough into a nice, smooth ball.

"Plastic wrap, please, Noelle," her grandmother said, and Noelle found the wrap in the cabinet, tore off a piece, and then wrapped it around the ball of dough. Grandma Ruth put it in the fridge as Noelle cleaned out the mixing bowl, and then they got to work on the next batch of cookies.

A few hours later the table was piled with sugar cookies, peanut butter cookies, and chocolate thumbprints.

"Time for a break," Grandma Ruth said. "I made egg salad for lunch. We can eat in the living room. Can you set up the tables?"

Noelle fetched two little folding tables from the closet in the living room; her grandmother always called them "TV tables." As she set them up in front of the green flowered couch, she became distracted by one of the photos on the side table: a black-and-white photo of two teenagers. Noelle picked it up and studied it for a minute. The girl's thick hair was pulled back in a ponytail, and she wore a button-down shirt, a wide knee-high skirt, and black-and-white shoes. The boy's hair looked like it was slicked back with gel, and he wore a short-sleeved shirt tucked into neatly pressed slacks.

"Is that you and Grandpa Everett?" Noelle asked as her grandmother entered with a tray of sandwiches and iced tea.

Grandma Ruth nodded. "It certainly is. Wasn't he handsome?" she replied with a little sigh. Grandpa Everett had died four years ago, and Noelle still missed him. She knew her grandma must miss him even more.

"You were so young when you met," Noelle remarked.

"We were even younger than that," her grandmother said. "We were in middle school. About your age, I think."

Noelle was interested. "Really?"

"Yes, and I'll never forget it," Grandma Ruth said. "I was walking to school, and it was raining, and I slipped on some wet leaves and my lunch bag fell in a puddle. Not only did your grandfather help me up, but he gave me his cheese sandwich, too. I think I fell in love with him that very day."

Noelle couldn't help thinking of Noel. That sounded like something he would do.

"Put down that picture and let's eat," Grandma Ruth said. "We've still got cookies to bake! We've got to do the gingerbread, and the jam tarts, and the pinwheels . . ."

Noelle knew they had a lot of work ahead of them, but she didn't mind. It was fun, and besides—it was a good way to stop thinking about Noel every second!

chapter 10

"NOELLE, YOU AND YOUR GRANDMA MAKE THE BEST cookies," Hailey said, biting into a snowman-shaped sugar cookie.

"Thanks," Noelle said. "She sent me home with so many bags of them, I can bring in a new one every day."

The friends sat at their table in the lunchroom, happily munching on Christmas cookies.

"I'm so psyched for your party Saturday," Alyson said. "What kind of food are you having?"

"We're doing six-foot heroes, one regular and one with eggplant for the vegetarians," Noelle reported. "And my dad is making a bunch of appetizers."

"Thanks for the vegetarian stuff," Hailey said. "Otherwise my mom said she would send over a plate of tofu balls."

"That's why we ordered the eggplant," Noelle teased.

"Hey, I like those tofu balls!" Hailey protested.

"Remember the last time we had them?" Jess asked. "We ended up playing tofu ball ping-pong."

"Well, there won't be any ping-pong at this party," Noelle said. "Or tofu balls. We're also having an amazing birthday cake. It's going to be vanilla with chocolate filling and white icing with violet sprinkles on it."

Hailey held up an imaginary slice of birthday cake to her mouth and pretended to eat it. "*Nom nom nom*. I could eat birthday cake every day."

Noelle scrolled to the list she had made on her phone.

"I have the music playlist all set, and Mom told Andrew that he has to lend us his player for the party," Noelle continued. "I still have to put the favors in the bags. And tonight Mom is taking me and Alyson to get my dress."

"I'm so psyched!" Alyson said. "I found a version of the violet dress on the Teen City website, and I called the mall and they said they have a bunch on the rack."

"Ooh, I can't wait to see it!" Hailey squealed. "Can we come over tomorrow? I can't wait until the party."

Noelle turned to Jess. "Do you have basketball practice tomorrow?"

Jess shook her head. "Nope, I'm good. We should all come over."

"Yeah, there's hardly any homework this time of year anyway," Hailey pointed out.

"I'll ask my mom," Noelle said.

The next day after school the four girls gathered in Noelle's room. Hailey picked up one of the snow globes.

"These are so pretty," Hailey said. "Each one is like its own little magical world."

"I can't believe every room in your house is decorated for Christmas," Alyson said, looking around.

"Not *every* room," Noelle corrected her. "The family room is totally reserved for my party."

Hailey sat on the bed and started to bounce up and down. "The dress! The dress! Let's see the dress!"

"Wait till you see it," Alyson said. "It's gorgeous."

"Okay, okay." Noelle opened the closet and pulled out the dress. "Ta-da!"

The dress was violet, of course, with a straight neckline, little capped sleeves, and a skirt with a tiny bit of a poof on the bottom.

"Isn't it beautiful?" Alyson asked. "You are going to look so pretty."

Jess nodded. "That's really nice."

"Thanks," Noelle said. "The only problem is that I'm not sure what to wear with it. I mean, I don't think I have any shoes that go with it."

Alyson grinned and opened the duffel bag she was carrying. "Don't worry, I've got it," she said. "I went to four Bat Mitzvahs last year, and you have to get dressed up for each one, so I have a ton of stuff."

She pulled out a pair of glittery silver flats. "The silver goes great with the violet, and flats are good so that you can dance and your feet won't hurt. And we're the same size."

Noelle kicked off her boots and tried them on. "Perfect!"

Then Alyson held up some silver bangle bracelets and a silver necklace with a heart-shaped crystal on the end. "Your accessories should be silver too. But you should try everything on with the dress."

"Yay!" Noelle cried. "I'll change in the bathroom."

She grabbed everything and left the room. A few minutes later, she came out wearing the dress, the jewelry, and the shoes.

"You look like a princess!" Hailey exclaimed.

Jess nodded. "That looks great. You should become a professional stylist or something, Alyson."

"That's what my mom says," Alyson said, pleased.

"Thank you so much, Alyson. I could have never done this on my own."

Jess walked behind Noelle. "Maybe you should wear your hair up," she said, showing her.

"I almost forgot! I have a headband," Alyson said, ruffling through the duffle bag. She slipped a thin silver headband studded with clear jewels through Noelle's hair. Her dark curls fell into place around it."

"That is so cool," Hailey said. "It's like your princess crown."

Noelle looked into the mirror, feeling excited. "This is the perfect outfit for my first real birthday party."

"Especially since Noel will be there," Jess teased.

"That's right!" Hailey remembered. "Are you going to get him under the mistletoe? 'Cause there's mistletoe all over your house, so that should be easy."

Noelle blushed. "I don't want to kiss him! I just . . . like him," she admitted. She had never said it out loud before, and it felt weird.

"We knew that already," Jess said.

"Yeah, it's pretty obvious," Alyson agreed.

Noelle sat down. "My gosh! Do you think he knows?"

"Probably," Jess said matter-of-factly. "Since you stare at him like you're in a trance whenever you see him."

Noelle buried her face in her hands. "I knew it! He probably hates me."

"He wouldn't be coming to your party if he hated you," Jess pointed out.

"Yeah, he would have said no," Hailey said.

Noelle realized they were right. "That makes sense. Now can we talk about something else, please?"

"You mean how you're going to do the Snowflake Run with me on Thursday?" Jess asked.

"Oh, yeah, that's right," Noelle said.

"Ugh! I hate running. We do enough of that in gym," Alyson said.

"Yeah, it's always so cold," Hailey added.

"You guys are wimps," Jess said. "It's totally fun. They close down all of Main Street, and then we all get hot cocoa at the bakery when it's over."

"I can still get hot cocoa without running a mile," Alyson pointed out.

Jess turned to Noelle. "Come on, you need to run with me. It'll be good training if you're going to try out for track in the spring."

"But the tryouts are three months away," Noelle said.

"Well, how about running off all those holiday cookies we've been eating?" Jess asked.

Noelle laughed. "That's probably a good idea."

"You could work those cookies off in a nice, warm gym," Hailey pointed out.

Jess sighed. "Okay. I know one reason you definitely can't argue with. You know that *Noel* will probably be there."

Noelle smiled. "Okay. I'll go."

Jess laughed, shaking her head. "I knew it! But I don't care why you're going, as long as you're going to run with me."

Alyson shooed her off the bed. "Go take off that dress before it gets wrinkled."

Noelle jumped up and ran out of the room, giggling. Her party was only four days away, and it was going to be perfect!

chapter 11

THE NIGHT OF THE SNOWFLAKE RUN WAS CLEAR and cold, just above freezing. Noelle had on leggings, a T-shirt, a sweatshirt, and gloves, because she didn't want to run in a heavy coat. She ran to the car, shivering the whole way.

"Thanks for taking me, D-d-dad," Noelle said, dramatically chattering as she slipped her seat belt on.

"I haven't done a run like this in awhile," Mr. Winters replied. "It should be fun."

Cars crowded the municipal parking lot off Main Street, but Mr. Winters found a space. They quickly walked to Main Street, where giant lighted snowflakes shone on every telephone pole along the route. The storefronts were all decorated for the holidays, and Christmas carols blared over a loudspeaker attached to a police van by the starting line.

Spectators lined up on along the street, looking snug in puffy coats and mittens, and Noelle was jealous of them. She jogged in place, trying to keep warm, when Jess ran up to her.

"Come on, let's find a place at the starting line," she said, grabbing Noelle by the arm.

Mr. Winters nodded to them as he stretched. "I'll be running with the old people," he joked. "Be careful, and I'll meet you by the bakery after the race," he said. "Don't go wandering off anywhere."

"I won't, Dad!" Noelle called behind her as Jess dragged her off.

It looked to Noelle like at least a hundred runners had taken a place behind the starting line, which had been painted on the street in a red-and-white candy cane stripe.

"At least it's warmer in the middle of the crowd," Noelle said, rubbing her gloved hands together.

"We'll warm up when we run," Jess promised.

"I hope that's soon," Noelle said.

Then the Christmas music stopped and a woman's voice came over the speakers.

"Good evening, everyone. I am Mayor Sherman," she

said. "Welcome to our fifteenth annual Snowflake Run!"

The crowd cheered, and Jess grinned at Noelle.

"Remember, there are no winners or losers at the Snowflake Run," Mayor Sherman went on. "This is a race about holiday cheer! At the end of the race there is free cocoa for all in front of Tamika's Bakery! Don't forget to step inside and try one of Tamika's famous snowball cupcakes. And now, without further ado, let the race begin!"

A small cannon on the police van went off, sprinkling the runners with tiny fake snowflakes. With a cheer, the runners surged forward.

Jess flashed Noelle a smile as they joined the pack. The black sky above glittered with stars, and Noelle felt like she was in the middle of something magical.

She turned to look at a display in the candy shop window when she noticed a familiar head of wavy hair a few feet in front of her. Noel!

Without thinking, she quickened her pace to catch up with him.

Of course he's fast, Noelle thought. *He's Noel!*

But Noelle was fast too, and she jogged right up next to him and gave him a little wave.

"Hey!" he said, with a surprised grin. "I didn't know you were a runner!"

"For fun, mostly," Noelle said. "But I'm trying out for track this year."

"Me too," Noel said.

They fell into pace next to each other. For a while they were quiet, just looking at the decorations as they ran down the street.

"So, um, it's almost Christmas," Noelle said.

"The Snowflake Run kind of kicks off the last stretch until Christmas, don't you think?" Noel asked. "It'll be here before we know it."

"I can't wait," Noelle said. "I can't wait until Christmas break, either. But first Mr. Randinelli is giving us a big test. Can you believe it?"

Noel nodded. "I have him too. He's like Scrooge or something."

The effort of the run kept them quiet for the rest of the race, but Noelle cast a few sideways glances at him, not believing her luck. This really *was* a magical night.

The race took them to the end of Main Street, where they made a right turn into Pine Valley Park. Tamika's

Bakery sat right across from the park, and tables had been set up with big thermal containers of cocoa. To get there, they had to cross the finish line, which was marked by two old-fashioned lampposts wrapped in candy cane–striped ribbon.

Noelle took one step past the lampposts and then stopped, placing her hands on her knees.

"We did it!" she said, breathing heavily.

Noel high-fived her. "Awesome. Do you want to get some cocoa?"

Noelle was about to say yes when she suddenly remembered something—Jess! Frantically she looked behind at the runners coming up to the line, but didn't see her.

"I'm so sorry, I need to find Jess," Noelle said. "I guess I . . . I must have lost her. . . . I'll see you later!"

She hurried off, leaving Noel looking a little baffled. A huge rush of runners came through the finish line, and Noelle pushed through them until she spotted Jess.

"Jess! Jess!" Noelle yelled, waving her hand.

Jess walked up to her.

"I'm soooo sorry," Noelle said. "There's this big crowd, and . . ."

". . . and you had no problem finding Noel in it," Jess snapped. "I saw you."

Noelle felt terrible. "I just wanted to say hi. And then we were running, and . . ."

Jess rolled her eyes. "Whatever. Let's get cocoa."

"And then let me buy you a cupcake," Noelle said. "I owe you."

"Yes, you do," Jess agreed.

As they sipped their cups of hot cocoa, Noelle couldn't help glancing around to see if she could find Noel. Jess had every reason to be mad, but Noelle had been rude to Noel, also. What if he was mad at her too?

I probably blew it, Noelle thought. *There's no way that he'll come to my party now.*

Then she felt a hand on her shoulder.

"Nice run," her dad said. "I saw you moving fast."

Noelle gave Jess a pleading look, hoping her friend wouldn't say anything about why she was running fast. But Jess just smiled. "Hi, Mr. Winters. Noelle was just about to get me a cupcake."

"I'll get both of you a cupcake," Noelle's dad said. "My treat."

Tamika's snowball cupcakes were perfect little treats,

white cupcakes with rounded tops covered in fluffy white frosting, shredded coconut, and edible sparkles. Noelle bit into hers, but the sweetness took a backseat to her worries.

She felt bad for how she had treated Jess. She felt bad for how she handled Noel. It was a relief when her dad said it was time to go, and she bundled into the warm car.

"What's the matter, hon?" Mr. Winters asked as they drove home. "Tired?"

"No," Noelle said glumly. "It's just . . . I'm running out of holiday cheer, I guess."

Mr. Winters nodded. "The holiday season is wonderful, but it can also be stressful. Maybe the day after your party we'll just take some chill time, you know?"

Noelle nodded and stared at the window. Her holidays were starting to get stressful, for sure . . . but not for the usual reasons.

chapter 12

THE NEXT DAY, FRIDAY, WAS JUST ONE DAY before her party. Noelle was dying to talk about the party at lunch with her friends, but she noticed that Jess seemed quieter than usual.

She's probably mad about last night, Noelle guessed, but she didn't bring it up. Hailey and Alyson did most of the talking at lunch.

As soon as Noelle got home, she got right back into birthday mode.

"Okay," she announced at dinner, "I made a chart of everything that needs to get done tonight for the party."

"I have to go out for a bit after dinner, but I won't be long," Mr. Winters said.

"But my party is *tomorrow*," Noelle said. "As in, tonight is the last night we have to get ready for it. There's tons to do."

"I can help with whatever needs to be done," her mom said. "I've just got to bake some brownies for church Sunday morning, since I won't be able to do it tomorrow night. And Andrew can help too."

Andrew put down his fork. "Why do I have to help? It's her party."

Mrs. Winters gave him a *don't-mess-with-me* look. "Because we're a family and we help each other, that's why."

Noelle took her phone from her pocket and looked at the chart. "You can vacuum the rugs," she told her brother.

"No way am I taking orders from Sergeant Birthday over there," Andrew said, shaking his head. "That's just not right."

Mrs. Winters sighed. "Andrew, could you please vacuum? That's your job anyway. And when you're done I'll find something else for you to do."

Andrew rolled his eyes, but he didn't object, and went back to his plate of chicken.

"I won't be long, and then I'm going to make some cheese balls and some other appetizers," Mr. Winters said. "We've got all night."

Noelle sighed. "Fine."

"Well, it is the last weekend before Christmas," her mom pointed out. "It's normally a very busy weekend for us. But we're making it work. Your party's going to be lovely."

"Perfect," Noelle corrected her. "It's going to be perfect."

"Perfect is a tough word," Mr. Winters said. "You know, some artists and craftspeople intentionally put a mistake in everything they create. Some do it because they believe that no one or nothing can be perfect, and others think that it makes their works more interesting. So maybe you shouldn't aim for perfect."

"But I just don't want anything to go *wrong*," Noelle said. "What's so bad about that?"

"I think your father's got a point," Mrs. Winters said. "It can't hurt to relax a little bit. You'll probably have a better time."

"And so will *everyone* else," Andrew mumbled.

But the advice didn't sink in. Noelle was too excited. She kept picturing the party over and over again . . . guests arriving in the perfectly decorated room, and then Noel would enter, and smile at her, and Noelle would walk up to him, and . . .

"Noelle, are you listening?" her mom asked. "I was asking what you need me to do after I'm done baking."

"I still need to finish the favor bags," Noelle said. "And I was thinking of putting some of the extra violet flowers in the downstairs bathroom. And I want to set out the plates and cups and stuff."

Mrs. Winters nodded. "Okay, you do the plates and cups and I'll help with the favor bags when I'm done. I picked up a few more things yesterday."

"All right," Noelle said. "May I be excused, then?"

"Of course," Mr. Winters replied.

Noelle helped clear the kitchen after dinner, and a few hours later, the Winters house was a busy hub of activity. Mr. Winters had returned with packages that he whisked up to his bedroom, and was now sliding a pan of cheese balls into the oven. Andrew hid in his room for two hours, but now the sound of the vacuum blared through the house.

Mrs. Winters finished her brownies, and now she and Noelle were sitting at the kitchen table, filling the favor bags. Noelle had taken a lot of time picking out things that both kids and adults would like.

"Tiny box of chocolate. Check," Noelle said, putting

one in a violet bag. "Lip balm. Check. Violet pen. Check."

"And I found these," Mrs. Winters said, opening up a bag of tiny notebooks with silver covers, "to go with the pens."

"They're perfect!" Nicole exclaimed. "Am I allowed to say that?"

Mrs. Winters grinned. "I think that's all right."

Noelle filled a bag with all of the items and tied a silver ribbon to close it.

"You know what I like best about these?" Noelle asked.

"You mean besides the fact that they're perfect?" her mom replied, teasing.

"Yes," Noelle said. "I love them because there's nothing Christmasy in them!"

They finished the favor bags, dusted the furniture, and adjusted the decorations until Noelle was satisfied. When they were almost done, Mr. Winters came into the family room with a hand behind his back.

"I picked up something for you, almost-birthday girl," he said.

"What is it?" Noelle asked.

Mr. Winters held out his hand. "Ta-da!"

Noelle let out a shriek. "A violet lightbulb!"

"I could only find one," Mr. Winters said. "But I think it'll give you the effect you want."

"Let's put it in!" Noelle said, her green eyes shining with excitement.

Her dad screwed the bulb into the lamp next to the couch, and soon the room was bathed in a lovely purple glow.

"Ooh," Noelle breathed. "That really is perfect!"

She gazed around the room. Everything was just as she had imagined.

"Noelle, I have to admit, it does look pretty perfect," Mr. Winters said, giving her a squeeze. Then he looked at his watch. "Hey, it's almost eleven. You should get a good night's sleep for your big day tomorrow."

"I don't think I can sleep," Noelle said. "This is even better than Christmas Eve."

"Wow. That's pretty good," Mr. Winters said. "But do me a favor and try, okay?"

"Okay, Dad," Noelle said. "And thanks."

A short while later, Noelle snuggled into bed and stared at the twinkling lights on her tree. She closed her eyes and drifted off, dreaming of her perfect party.

NOELLE WOKE UP THE NEXT MORNING, WIDE AWAKE and excited. Her party wasn't until the afternoon, but she still had to help set up the food, and get dressed, and . . .

She suddenly froze, listening. Everything was so quiet. Too quiet. The kind of quiet you only hear . . . she ran to the window, her heart beating.

Snow blanketed everything she could see. It was piled up on the roof, mounded on the front lawn, and huge hills of it covered the street outside. There were no cars moving down the street, no people outside—just snow, snow, snow everywhere she looked. Heavy white flakes were pouring from the sky. That's why it was so quiet.

Normally, Noelle loved snow, especially on Christmas. But none of her birthday dreams had included snow.

Panicked, she ran downstairs. Her mom and dad

were awake, drinking coffee in the kitchen and wearing bathrobes. They stared at the small kitchen TV with worried looks on their faces.

"What's going on?" Noelle asked.

Her mom looked at her with a sympathetic frown. "Oh, honey, it's a record-breaking blizzard."

"A blizzard?" Noelle asked. "I didn't even know it was going to snow!"

Her parents looked at each other. "Well, yesterday they were predicting three inches, so we weren't too worried about it," Mr. Winters said. "We didn't tell you because we didn't want you to worry either."

Noelle looked out the back door. The snow was piled as high as the porch railing. She hadn't seen anything like it in years.

"So people can still come, right?" she asked, her voice shaking a little.

"There's a state of emergency," her mom replied. "They're asking people to stay inside because the roads aren't safe. Some people don't even have power. I'm so sorry, honey, but we have to cancel the party."

"Nooooooo!" Noelle wailed. "The party's not till five. The roads will be clear by then, won't they?"

Mr. Winters shook his head. "This is a big storm, honey. It could take days before the roads are clear."

"But it's not fair!" Noelle cried, and then before she could explode into tears, she ran up to her room, slamming the door behind her.

"Stupid snow," she mumbled, burying her face in her pillow. She felt hot tears sting her eyes, and she struggled to hold them back. She didn't want to end up like one of those girls on *Sixteen and Spoiled* who burst into tears when the balloons were the wrong color or they didn't get the deejay they wanted.

But at least they all got their parties, she thought miserably. *I don't even get to have mine!*

A knock sounded on the door. "Come in," Noelle called out meekly.

"It's me," her mom said. "Is it okay if I go to your invitation site and send out an e-mail about the party? Just to make sure nobody is worried about getting here."

"Fine," Noelle said flatly.

"Okay then. Dad's starting breakfast," Mrs. Winters said in a quiet voice, and then she left.

Noelle took her time getting dressed, only heading downstairs when the smell of bacon was too hard to resist. She carried her laptop with her. Her parents didn't normally let her use it at the table, but she had a feeling that they wouldn't object today.

She was right. As she sat down and opened her laptop, her dad slid a plate of pancakes and bacon in front of her.

"I'm just going to see if anybody replied to the e-mail yet," Noelle said.

"That's fine, honey," her dad said.

"I just sent out the e-mail," her mom said. "So people might not be replying just yet."

But Noelle found a bunch of replies waiting for her on the site. The first was from Hailey.

Noooooooo! Soooooo sooooorrrrrry!

Alyson wrote next.

That stinks! But you still have to wear your dress today, no matter what.

Noelle wanted to smile at that, but couldn't just yet. She got a few other replies from kids who were sorry, and her cousin Nick was psyched that he might have a snow day Monday.

Then, to her surprise, she saw a reply from Noel.

> You must be so disappointed. But hope you enjoy
> the snow day and have a great birthday.

Noelle sighed. Leave it to Noel to send a perfect reply. Then she realized, with horror, that her mother was looking over her shoulder.

"That Noel seems like such a nice boy," she said.

"He is," Noelle replied, willing herself not to blush. Then she shut her laptop and picked up a piece of bacon.

The reply from Noel helped her feel a little better. How sweet was he? But she hadn't seen anything from Jess. Was her friend still mad at her? She must be, if she didn't reply, Noelle reasoned, and that thought put her in a bad mood again.

Mr. Winters put his coffee cup in the sink and stretched. "Well, at least the snow has stopped. I guess I should get to shoveling the walk—if I can find it."

"Andrew and I can help you," Mrs. Winters said, just

as Andrew appeared in the kitchen, yawning.

"Wait, why doesn't Noelle have to help?" Andrew asked.

Mrs. Winters just glared at him, and Andrew shrugged. Noelle was glad that they weren't asking her to help. She didn't feel like going outside in all that stupid party-ruining snow. In fact, she didn't even feel like changing out of her pajamas.

Without a word, she got up and put her breakfast dishes in the sink and headed up to her room. Her parents didn't ask any questions.

Noelle had never felt so "blah" in her life. She climbed into bed, pulled up the covers, and opened her laptop again. For a few minutes she just stared at Noel's reply. She checked her e-mail again, hoping to hear from Jess, but there was nothing. Worried, Noelle texted her.

RU ok? No party today. ⊗ Wish u were here.

She waited a few minutes for the little beep of Jess's return text, but it never came. Then, bored, she went back to the laptop and clicked on a computer game where she shot rainbow bubbles out of the sky with lemons over and over and over again. After a while her hand got stiff and she found herself squinting at the screen, so she reluctantly got out of bed.

She showered and dressed in pink leggings and a sweatshirt, putting on her favorite pair of fluffy slippers. Then her mom knocked on the door and came in, smiling when she saw Noelle.

"Andrew took a walk and said everyone's sledding over at the hill on Mill Street," her mom reported. "Want to go?"

Noelle shook her head. "No thanks."

Her mom didn't push it. "Okay, then. We'll be back soon. I don't know how many times I can go up and down that hill."

Listless for the rest of the day, Noelle read a few chapters of a book she was in the middle of; played a few more games on her laptop; and rearranged her sweater drawer, organizing everything by color. She checked her e-mail a few times, but Jess never replied, and that just put her in a bad mood all over again.

She didn't join her parents and Andrew for cocoa when they got back from sledding. But when Mr. Winters called up that it was time to eat, Noelle's empty stomach led her down the stairs.

The kitchen table was laden with all kinds of food: veggies and dip, chips, deviled eggs, little cucumber sandwiches, and her dad's famous cheese balls.

"I made all this for your party yesterday," Mr. Winters explained. "And I'd hate for it to go to waste. Besides, I thought it would be kind of fun, right?"

"I guess so," Noelle said. It definitely was more interesting than sitting down to a regular dinner. But at the same time, it made her a little sad, thinking about all her family and friends who weren't going to get to eat it.

Andrew piled a mound of cheese balls on his plate. "I could eat like this every day," he remarked. "After this I want to head back to the hill. Josh is putting oil on the bottom of his sled and that thing's going to go down that hill like crazy."

"We might have something to do right after dinner," Mrs. Winters said, with what she hoped was a secret nod toward Noelle, who was absently peeling apart the strands of a celery stalk and didn't notice.

Andrew rolled his eyes. "Yeah. Whatever."

As they were finishing, Noelle's mom got up from the table. Suddenly, the lights went out and Mrs. Winters came in carrying a cake with twelve candles, one extra for good luck, and HAPPY BIRTHDAY NOELLE written in violet icing.

"*Happy birthday to you . . .*" she began to sing, and Mr. Winters and Andrew joined in.

That's when it hit her. The river of tears she'd been holding back all day broke through, and she started to cry. As her family's voices trailed off, she ran up to her room.

She flopped down on the bed, sobbing. This wasn't how it was supposed to be! She knew it was nobody's fault, but still, why did it have to snow on *her* day? Her one special day?

It was supposed to be perfect! Noelle thought, burying her head in her pillow.

chapter 14

NOELLE CRIED UNTIL SHE HAD NO MORE TEARS.
Her face felt hot, and she lay on her back for a while,
staring at the ceiling, until she heard a knock on the door.

To her surprise, it was Andrew, carrying a big box
wrapped in pink paper.

"I was going to save this for your real birthday, but I'm
thinking you might need something to cheer you up right
now," he said.

Noelle sat up, surprised. "Really?"

"Yeah, why not?" Andrew replied with a shrug. Noelle
had almost forgotten how nice her brother could be when
he wanted to.

She took the box from him. The wrapping was
bunched in places, so she could tell that he had done it
himself. He had even tied a lopsided purple ribbon around
the box.

"What is it?" she asked.

Andrew grinned. "Open it and see."

Noelle carefully unwrapped the paper and then lifted the lid of the box to see a pair of pale pink ice skates inside.

"Oh my gosh! These are exactly the ones I wanted!" she cried, picking up one of the skates.

"Well, I want to race you this year, and now that you have new skates there's no excuse if you lose," Andrew teased.

Noelle laughed. Every year, the Winters went ice skating on Christmas Day. She had outgrown her skates from last year, and had been looking at new ones for the last few months. And of course the fact that they were pink was just . . . perfect.

She pushed the box aside and jumped up to hug Andrew. "Thank you! This is awesome. But why didn't you wait until my birthday?"

"I guess I just was thinking that it must kind of stink to open birthday presents and Christmas presents on the same day," her brother replied. "You probably never even remember which are the birthday ones and which are the Christmas ones. But maybe you'll remember this time.

And it stinks that your party was canceled."

"Yeah, it does stink," Noelle agreed. "So I guess I will definitely race you on Christmas then. And these skates look pretty fast."

"Yeah, well, good luck," Andrew said with a grin.

He left the room, leaving the door open. Noelle could hear music playing downstairs. She felt pretty bad about running out on her birthday cake, so she wiped the last stray tear from her eye and made her way downstairs.

She found everyone in the family room, which was still decorated for the party. A cozy fire crackled in the fireplace.

"Hey," Noelle said. Her parents looked relieved to see her.

"You okay, honey?" her mom asked, putting an arm around her.

Noelle nodded. "Yeah. I didn't mean to freak out like that, it's just . . ."

"It's okay, we know," her mom assured her.

"Does this mean we can hit the rewind button?" Mr. Winters asked.

Noelle nodded. "Sure."

Her dad left the room, Andrew hit the lights, and

Mr. Winters came back in with the birthday cake.

"Happy birthday, birthday girl!" her parents shouted, and they were so dorky that Noelle couldn't help laughing. Then Andrew joined in as they sang the birthday song.

"Okay, make a wish!" Mr. Winters cried.

Noelle closed her eyes. *Since there was no party, please let me see Noel again, somewhere else, soon,* she thought.

It was kind of an odd wish, she knew, but she opened her eyes and blew out the candles all at once.

"Hooray!" her mom cried. "That means your wish will come true."

"I hope so," Noelle said.

"Hey, anybody want to play Monopoly?" her dad asked.

"Sure," Andrew said.

"I thought you were going sledding?" Noelle asked.

Andrew shrugged. "Josh's mom won't let him oil the sled. She says it's too dangerous."

"Well, it is," Mrs. Winters agreed.

"Are we going to play Monopoly or what?" Andrew asked.

"Yes!" Noelle said, heading to the table. She picked

up her carefully placed table decorations and moved them out of the way.

They played the game, laughing, and Andrew kept getting up to go outside and take pictures of the snow with his phone.

"It's really cool with the moon shining on it and stuff," he reported. "And it's, like, more snow than I've ever seen in my life."

Mrs. Winters won the game (*as usual,* Noelle thought), and then Noelle put on the Holiday Channel just as *A Christmas Story* was coming on.

"Are you sure you want to watch a Christmas movie tonight?" her mom asked. "It's still your birthday-only celebration, if you want it to be."

"It's okay. It seems like the right thing to do, with all the snow outside," Noelle said.

"Plus it's an awesome movie," Andrew added.

"You know what else is awesome?" Mr. Winters asked. "S'mores!"

"S'mores in winter?" Noelle wondered.

"Why not?" her dad replied. "We've got marshmallows and chocolate and graham crackers. And fire." He waved his arm at the fireplace.

"What'll we use for sticks?" Noelle asked.

"I was thinking my long barbecue fork," he answered. "We'd have to do one marshmallow at a time, but that's okay."

Noelle nodded. "Let's do it!"

Her dad's plan actually worked out perfectly. Noelle snuggled on the couch next to her mom and watched the movie, while Andrew sprawled out on the loveseat and her dad pulled a chair up to the fireplace, making s'mores one by one and delivering them.

"First one goes to the birthday girl," he said with a grin.

Noelle bit into the warm, gooey treat, and some of the melted marshmallow squeezed out of the side, but that's what always happened when she ate a s'more. She caught the stray marshmallow with her tongue.

"Yum! Dad, this is awesome," Noelle said.

At that moment she realized that it was a pretty good night, after all. She looked up at her mom.

"Thanks, Mom," she said. "This is really nice."

Her mother stroked her hair. "Nothing ever goes perfectly as planned, sweetie," she said. "But usually things end up working out."

"They do," Noelle agreed. Tonight wasn't the perfect

party she had planned, but it was perfect in its own way.

When the movie finished, Noelle headed to bed. She checked her e-mail and phone one last time, but there was still nothing from Jess. She started to feel a little sad again, so she looked at the message from Noel.

> You must be so disappointed. But hope you enjoy the snow day and have a great birthday.

"Thanks, Noel," she whispered. "I had a terrible birthday party, but I did have a great snow day."

THE NEXT MORNING DAWNED COLD AND SUNNY.
Outside the window, Noelle could see the snow piled up
in mounds on the street. The snowplows hadn't even
reached them yet.

Now that the disappointment of the canceled party
had faded a little, Noelle started to feel appreciation for
the day ahead. It was kind of nice not to be able to go
anywhere; she could relax and finish up her Christmas
stuff, and even stay in her pj's all day if she wanted.

The night before, Noelle had put on a pair of pink
flannel pajamas with snowflakes, and she thought they
were the most comfortable thing in the world. She put on
her slippers and went downstairs for breakfast.

Her mom and dad were at the table, drinking coffee.

"Dad's going to make omelets this morning,"
Mrs. Winters reported. "What do you want in yours?"

"I found mushrooms, green peppers, and some Swiss cheese in the fridge," her dad said.

Noelle grinned. "Yes!"

She went to the refrigerator to get the orange juice, when the front doorbell rang.

"Who's that?" she wondered out loud. "Did Andrew go out this morning?"

Her mom shook her head. "No, he's still sleeping. Why don't you see who it is?"

Curious, Noelle went to the door and looked through the little window there.

"Jess!" she shrieked.

She quickly unlocked the door and pulled Jess inside. Her friend was bundled up in a parka and striped scarf, and her cheeks were red.

"What are you doing here? Why didn't you call me?" Noelle asked.

Jess stomped her boots on the floor mat to get the snow off. "We don't have power," she said. "Dad put the woodstove on, so we've been warm, and if it's not fixed today we're going to my aunt's house. So I didn't get your message about the party. Hailey walked over yesterday and told me. I felt so bad for you!"

"Thanks," Noelle said. "I texted you and you didn't text back, so I thought you were mad at me. For the Snowflake Run."

"I was kind of mad," Jess admitted. "But not enough to quit talking to you or anything. Especially since your party got canceled. I know you were probably so upset, especially after all that planning."

"I was, but I still feel bad about the run the other night," Noelle said. "I totally ignored you, and I'm really sorry."

"It's okay," Jess replied. Then she grinned. "I'm sure Noel's dazzling smile is just too hard to resist."

Noelle giggled. "It's true. When I'm around him it's like I'm in a stupid trance or something."

"Is that Jess?" Mrs. Winters called from the kitchen. "Bring her in here. Dad's making her an omelet."

"Awesome!" Jess said. "Walking in the snow made me superhungry."

Jess took off her coat, slipping a small package wrapped in purple paper out of her pocket.

"Happy birthday," she said.

Noelle hugged her. "Thanks! Come on, let's eat and I'll open it."

"Jess, how nice of you to walk all the way here,"

Mrs. Winters said. "Did I hear you say there's no power at your house?"

"It's supposed to come back on this morning," Jess reported.

"Jess, do you want mushrooms, peppers, and cheese in your omelet?" Mr. Winters asked over his shoulder.

"Just cheese, please," Jess said.

"You got it!"

Noelle unwrapped the little purple box Jess had given her and opened the lid. Inside was a pair of earrings with dangling purple and pink glass stones.

"Jess, these are perfect!" Noelle said, taking one out of the box.

"I looked really hard to find violet beads that would go with your dress," Jess explained. "I'm sorry you didn't get to wear it."

"It's okay," Noelle said. "These are my favorite colors. I can wear them anytime."

"You can still wear your dress on Christmas Eve," Mrs. Winters pointed out. "It will be lovely."

"Hey, I never thought of that," Noelle realized.

Mr. Winters slid a plate in front of each girl. "Dig in!"

The girls hungrily ate their omelets, not saying much

while they ate. When they finished, they went up to Noelle's room.

"Can you stay awhile?" Noelle asked.

"I have to be home by lunch," Jess replied. "But I can hang out until then."

Noelle looked down at her pj's.

"Um, let me go change."

She put on jeans and a purple shirt to match the earrings, and then came back to the room and put them in. The shiny glass gems sparkled in her dark curls.

"Those are so beautiful," Noelle said. "You should become a jewelry designer."

"Wait till you see what I made you for Christmas," Jess said, her eyes shining, and Noelle felt a sudden pang. She still hadn't made Jess's present!

"I can't wait," Noelle said. "Hey, you have to see this video of kittens I found yesterday!"

"Yay! Technology!" Jess said. "I can't wait until my power comes back on."

They settled on the rug and watched funny videos for a while, laughing like crazy, just like they always did when they got together. Before they knew it, it was time for Jess to leave.

Noelle hugged her when she was all bundled up and ready to go.

"I can't believe you have to walk all the way home again in the snow," she said.

"It's all right," Jess said, clutching a big thermos of soup that Mrs. Winters sent with her for the rest of her family. "It's good training for track practice. See you tomorrow. If we have school that is."

"See you," Noelle replied.

As soon as Jess left, Noelle ran upstairs. She had to make that present! She opened up her closet and pulled out the plastic bin with her sewing stuff. Grandma Ruth had taught her how to sew by hand when she was eight, and one of their favorite things to do was make little stuffed monsters and creatures out of felt. After pulling out the sewing box the other day, Noelle had been thinking about maybe making a special monster for Jess. She opened the lid of the box, hoping she had everything she needed.

She pulled out several sheets of felt in a bunch of colors, and there were scraps of material from some other projects she had made, and the little jar of buttons her grandmother had given her. And of course she had a tomato-shaped pincushion with needles and pins stuck in it, and a few different colors of thread.

Noelle sat down at her desk and drew a pattern on a piece of paper. The creature she had imagined for Jess would have a nice round head, pointy ears, a squat body, and a tail. Jess loved blue and orange, so she cut the monster's body out of blue felt and cut out some big orange eyes, and little orange triangles to go inside the ears.

Then she sewed the body, leaving some space so she could fill it with the white fluffy stuff the craft store sold for stuffing things. After it was filled, she sewed the opening shut, and then got to work on adding the finishing touches.

She sewed little black buttons inside the orange eye circles, and gave the mouth a little red tongue sticking out. For a finishing touch she made a little orange basketball out of felt and sewed it to the end of the tail.

"Sooooo cute!" Noelle said, holding the creature out in front of her as her mom walked by the door.

"So that's what you've been doing up here," Mrs. Winters said. "That's adorable!"

"It's Jess's Christmas present," Noelle told her. "I've been meaning to work on it for weeks. And now Christmas is almost here."

"I know," Mrs. Winters said. "It's going to be a busy

week. We'll need to hold on to our Santa hats!"

Noelle's mom was right. The week before Christmas went by in a blur. Noelle hoped she'd run into Noel but everyone was superbusy. Monday night they all went to see the Winter Concert at the high school, because Andrew played trombone in the concert band. Noelle couldn't believe how grown-up he looked in his white shirt and black tie.

On Tuesday, Noelle wrapped all of her presents. Wednesday, she helped her mom bake two pies for Christmas. Thursday was a half day, and Grandma Ruth picked Noelle up from school. Then they drove around to all of her grandmother's friends, delivering boxes of the cookies they had made. Noelle always liked this part of Christmas.

"What a beautiful granddaughter!" they would say.

And Grandma Ruth would always reply, "She gets it from me."

All week long, Noelle thought of her birthday wish. All she wanted to do was run into Noel so she could wish him a happy birthday, and maybe talk to him a little bit. But she didn't see him all week.

Friday was another half day. The morning flew by;

they didn't do any work in their classes. In science class they watched a video about polar bears, and in English class they basically just had a little party. Each time the bell rang, Noelle hurried into the hall, hoping to catch Noel passing by, but she didn't see him.

When the final bell rang, she waited in the front hall, watching everyone head out. The bus was going to leave in a minute, she knew, but she couldn't bear the thought of leaving without seeing Noel before Christmas.

Mr. Clark walked up as she stood in the near-empty hallway.

"Hurry, Noelle," he said. "You don't want to get stuck here for winter break all by yourself!"

Noelle smiled. "Thanks, Mr. Clark." She cast one last look down the hall, sighed, and then ran out to get the bus.

When she got home, she opened up her laptop. She didn't get to wish Noel a happy birthday in person, but she could do the next best thing.

Subject: Happy Almost Birthday!

Hope you have a happy birthday tomorrow. And a Merry Christmas, too! (Just not lumped together!)

She hit send and smiled as she imagined Noel opening it up. Then she turned on the lights on her tiny Christmas tree. It blinked, making the whole room pretty. The house smelled delicious. Her family was all home and getting ready for dinner. And Jess wasn't angry at her.

She didn't get her party. She didn't get her wish. It wasn't perfect, but that was all right.

Christmas was almost here!

chapter 16

"SILENT NIGHT, HOLY NIGHT . . ."

Noelle stared at the candles flickering on the altar of the darkened church as she sang along to the hymn. This was always her favorite moment in the Christmas Eve service, when there didn't seem to be another sound in the world except the beautiful, clear voices of the singers. The peace of the moment seemed to fill up her whole body, and she closed her eyes, savoring it.

Then she glanced down the pew at her family: her mom and dad, Andrew, Grandma Ruth, and her aunt Emily and cousin Nick, who joined them on Christmas Eve every year. A few rows ahead she saw Jess with her parents and two brothers. There was something really comforting about being surrounded by all the people she loved best.

The hymn ended, and they sat down as Reverend Bailey

read a final prayer. Noelle felt her mind drift briefly to Noel. Was he in a church somewhere too, singing the same hymns? Or home, blowing out candles on a birthday cake?

Then the organ blared a rousing chord, and everyone stood up and started talking and hugging each other. Jess wiggled her way through the crowded aisle to see her.

"Cool, you wore the dress!" Jess said, looking at her. "It really is pretty."

"I had to," Noelle said, looking down at her violet party dress. "Hey, take a picture so we can show Alyson."

Jess took out her phone and Noelle did a quick pose. Then she put on her coat and they followed the crowd outside.

Noelle shivered. The sky above was clear and filled with shining stars—a perfect Christmas Eve sky. A blanket of white snow still covered everything, too. She waved good-bye to Jess and ran to catch up to her family in their car.

The ride home from church was another of Noelle's favorite things about Christmas Eve. As they drove down the streets of Pine Valley, they looked at all the lights and decorations, everything from simple candles in a window to giant, inflated, smiling Santas. The Winters family always played a little game: find the best-decorated house.

"*That's* the best house," Noelle said, pointing to one with light-up candy canes lining the walkway.

Then they passed a house with what looked like dozens of lighted snowmen on the lawn. "No, *that* one's the best," Andrew said.

"That's pretty good," Noelle admitted, so she scanned the street to find the next best one. They stopped at a traffic light, and on the corner a house had an entire Santa's workshop on the lawn, complete with elves and toys. An inflatable Santa watched over the whole thing, checking his list.

"*That's* the best one!" Noelle cried, pointing.

"No way. The snowman one was better," Andrew countered.

Noelle leaned toward the front seat. "Which one was better?" she asked her parents.

"I think the toy shop," Mr. Winters said, and his wife nodded.

"Yes, the toy shop," Mrs. Winters agreed.

Noelle clapped. "Yes!"

"I'll find a better one," Andrew said, but even though they saw many beautiful houses on the way home, nothing beat the Santa's workshop house.

When they reached home, Aunt Emily and Nick were waiting in the driveway for them, along with Grandma Ruth. They hurried into the house, shivering.

"All right, Winters family," Mr. Winters called out. "Christmas mode!"

Noelle knew just what to do. They'd had the same tradition ever since they could remember. She unwrapped a cookie platter and brought it into the family room, while Mr. Winters made cocoa, Andrew put out a plate of vegetables and dip, and Mrs. Winters put the finishing touches on a sandwich platter.

Noelle turned on the lights on the special Christmas tree that they had bought for the family room that morning. It was small, like the one in her bedroom, and Noelle had decorated it with purple and pink ornaments she had made herself, out of sparkly chenille sticks and craft paper. The family room was still decorated in birthday colors, but now it felt more like Christmas.

Mrs. Winters came in and turned on the Holiday Channel, where *It's a Wonderful Life* was just starting.

"This is my favorite Christmas movie," Grandma Ruth said, like she did every year. "It always makes me cry."

"Me too. But in a good way," Noelle said, snuggling up to her on the couch.

Even though they had all seen the movie a bunch of times, they were all quiet during most of it, except for the sounds of crunching carrots and slurping cocoa. Nick, who was eight, fell asleep on the rug. Aunt Emily, who had red hair just like Noelle's dad, gently woke him when the movie ended.

"Come on, Nick," she said. "We've got to beat Santa home."

Nick woke up, yawning. "Come on, let's hurry!" he said, and everyone laughed.

Aunt Emily gave Noelle a hug. "Happy almost birthday, sweetie. I'm sorry your party got canceled. You look so beautiful in your dress. And you'll look just as beautiful in it next month."

"Thanks," Noelle said. She had asked Mom about rescheduling the party, and Mrs. Winters had said that maybe they could do it in January. It wouldn't be the same, but it would still be special.

"Noelle, Andrew, I want you to get ready for bed now," Mrs. Winters said, yawning herself. "I know you're going to wake up early tomorrow."

Noelle didn't argue. She felt sleepy as soon as her head touched the pillow, and she had one last thought before she drifted off.

It really is a wonderful life, isn't it?

And it would be perfect if I could just see Noel. . .

chapter 17

AFTER WHAT SEEMED LIKE NO TIME AT ALL, NOELLE'S eyes flew open. She looked at her clock: 7:03. The house was quiet, which meant she was the first one awake.

She felt excited, and not sleepy at all. She climbed out of bed, put on her slippers, and tiptoed to Andrew's room.

"Andrew," she whispered, knocking on the door. "Come on, it's Christmas."

Her brother didn't reply, so she pushed the door open. "Andrew! It's Christmas!" she repeated, in a louder whisper this time.

"All right. One minute," her brother grumbled, and Noelle stepped back and waited in the hallway, impatiently tapping her slippered foot on the carpet. Finally Andrew emerged, his red hair tousled. After one year when Andrew went downstairs and opened all his presents before everyone else woke up, they now had a deal that they all went downstairs together.

They barged into their parents' bedroom, not even bothering to knock. Andrew flicked the light switch.

"It's Christmas!" Noelle shrieked.

Mr. Winters sat up, squinting. "What time is it?"

"It's after seven," Noelle answered. "That's late enough. Come on!"

"Okay," her mom said, her eyes still closed. "Just give us a minute to get ready."

Noelle and Andrew sat at the top of the stairs, waiting for what seemed like forever until their parents appeared.

"Let me just get the coffee on first," Mr. Winters pleaded.

"No!" Noelle cried. "Presents first!"

She bounded down the stairs, feeling exactly like she had on every Christmas morning she could remember. It was like that feeling when a candy cane first hit the tip of your tongue, or when a snowflake kissed your cheek, or when you saw a shooting star in the winter sky. She raced into the living room, where the presents had been placed under the big Christmas tree.

"Wait!" Mr. Winters cried. "Before presents, we have to do one very important thing."

"No coffee," Noelle said.

"No, not coffee," he said, grinning and opening his arms. "Happy birthday, Noelle!"

"Yes, happy birthday, sweetheart," her mom said, hugging her.

"Right. Happy birthday," Andrew added.

Noelle smiled. "Thanks, everybody. Now can we do presents?"

Mrs. Winters laughed. "Of course."

Noelle's job since she had been little was to deliver the presents under the tree to her parents and brother. As she went through the wrapped boxes, she couldn't help noticing that a lot of them had purple or pink paper.

"Oh my gosh!" Noelle exclaimed. "Uncle Marty and Aunt Ellen sent me two separate gifts this year. So did Grandpa Henry and Nana. And Aunt Jane, too."

"Well, it is your birthday *and* Christmas too, right?" Mr. Winters asked, with a twinkle in his eye. "Isn't that what you've been telling us all along?"

It wasn't long before all the gifts had been opened, even the birthday ones. Noelle loved opening her gifts, but even more she loved to see the expressions on the faces of her family when they opened theirs. Her mom opened a box from Noelle to find some spicy-smelling candles.

"I bought them at the craft fair," Noelle told her. "I thought they smelled nice."

"Oh, honey, they're lovely!" her mom said, picking one up.

Her dad loved the figurine of a Santa dressed like a chef that she had picked out for him—and the guitar-shaped spatula to go with it.

"I'll make totally rocking omelets now," he joked.

Andrew was always the hardest to get something for, but Noelle had saved up to get him a video game he really wanted.

"Thanks," Andrew said, and even though that's all he said, Noelle could tell he really liked it.

Then the phone rang, and Mrs. Winters nodded to Noelle.

"Can you get that, honey?" she asked.

"Sure." Noelle picked up the phone in the kitchen.

"Happy birthday!"

Noelle recognized her Aunt Jane's voice. "Thanks," she replied, "and merry Christmas!"

One by one her relatives called, and each one yelled

"Happy birthday!" right away. Only her Uncle Marty got a little mixed up.

"Merry birthday!" he yelled. "Oh, I mean, happy Christmas! I mean happy birthday! Happy birthday, Noelle!"

Noelle was laughing so hard.

"Did you ask everyone to wish me a happy birthday first today?" Noelle asked her mother, when all the calls were over.

Her mom gave her an innocent look. "Why would I do that, honey?" But Noelle didn't care what the reason was—it felt good.

Dad waved his new spatula. "I'm going to use this on the French toast," he announced.

"Can I go over to Jess's after breakfast?" Noelle asked. "I want to give her the gift I made."

Her mom looked at the clock. "We're heading to the pond around eleven thirty, so how about I pick you up from there?"

Noelle nodded. "Okay."

They ate a big breakfast of French toast and sausages and fruit, and then Noelle got changed into her skating outfit—pale pink leggings with a purple skating skirt over them and a purple sweater with little pink hearts. Her puffy white vest and pink gloves would keep her warm on the ice.

Jess was still in pajamas when Noelle got to her house.

"Merry Christmas!" Noelle cried.

"Happy birthday!" Jess yelled back.

Noelle stepped inside and took off her coat. "Aren't you going skating?"

"Soon," Jess said. "But James and Taylor got a new video game, and we've all been playing it." She nodded toward the living room, where her parents and two brothers were still in their pj's, laughing as they played the game. They paused briefly to wish Noelle a happy birthday, and then the girls went up to Jess's bedroom. Noelle promptly handed over the present.

"Open it!" she urged eagerly.

Jess ripped open the wrapping. "It's so cute!" she squealed. "I love her. I'm going to name her . . . Hoops!"

"Perfect!" Noelle said, and then Jess handed her a box to open. Inside was a little wooden box decorated with purple and pink gems.

"I make jewelry, so I might as well make jewelry boxes, too," she explained.

"This is awesome!" Noelle said. "I'm going to keep all

the jewelry you've ever made for me in it."

The girls sat in the room for a while, talking about what gifts they had gotten. Before Noelle knew it, her phone beeped.

"They're outside," Noelle said. "Gotta go."

"I think Hailey and Alyson are there already," Jess informed her. "Hopefully, I'll be there soon."

It wasn't a long trip to the skating pond, and soon Noelle was seated on a bench, lacing up her new pink skates.

"Perfect!" she said, smiling, and tying the final bow. Then she looked out at the pond.

Going ice skating on Christmas Day was a Winters family tradition, and a tradition for many people in Pine Valley, too. A shallow man-made pond maintained by the town, the rink hardened up nicely after a few days of sub-freezing weather. Skaters made their way around the circle in their colorful winter gear. Some went slowly, or held on tightly to their skating partner, while others effortlessly glided and twirled past her. A few little kids were just sitting on the ice. Gentle snow flurries danced in the air, making the whole scene prettier, like sprinkles on a cupcake.

She scanned the crowd, looking for Hailey and Alyson, when she spotted him . . . Noel! He wore a green-and-red sweater and he had that smile on his face that Noelle loved so much. His cheeks were pink from the cold, and his brown hair, dotted with snowflakes, was blowing in the wind.

He looks like a Christmas dream, Noelle thought. *Only he's real!*

She stepped onto the ice and, steadying herself, joined the flow of the crowd. Noel was up ahead, but then he rounded the curve . . . *he should be able to see me now, right?* Noelle wondered. *Should I wave? Call out his name?* She tried to skate a little faster, but she almost tripped. She quickly steadied herself, her heart pounding. She was a really good skater, and hadn't had a wipeout since she was a little kid.

She made her way around the pond again, still wondering what to do, when Noel's face lit up as he spotted her. He waved and then cut across the pond, skating toward her.

That's when Noelle noticed the girl skating just behind him. She had seen her before but now it was clear that she was definitely following Noel, not just some random skater behind him. A terrible thought hit her: Was she Noel's girlfriend?

But nobody had ever talked about Noel having a girlfriend. Unless it was a secret girlfriend? No, Noel wouldn't keep a secret like that. A cousin, maybe?

Oh, I hope it's his cousin! Noelle thought.

Noel skated in a circle around her. "Happy birthday!" he called out.

"Hi, Christmas Eve birthday boy!" Noelle called back. "Did you have a good birthday?"

"We did!" said the girl, startling Noelle a little. Did she mean that she had the same birthday as Noel?

Noel grinned. "This is my twin sister, Christina," he said, skating to a stop.

Noelle smiled shyly, trying not to stare. How did she *not* know that Noel had a twin sister?

"Hi!" the girl said brightly. She looked a lot like Noel, with the same sparkling brown eyes and brown hair and big smile. She had on a pink skating skirt and white leggings—and pink skates.

"We have the same skates," Christina said, pointing.

"We totally do! I just got them for my birthday," Noelle said. Then she turned to Noel. "I didn't know you had a twin!"

"I go to a different school!" Christina said loudly, and

Noelle realized that she spoke a little slowly, too. "I go to the Orchard School."

Noelle nodded. The Orchard School was a school for special-needs kids.

"I like it there!" Christina said, beaming.

"It looks nice," Noelle told her. "They have that great playground, right?" The school chorus had performed there once, and Noelle had always remembered the playground. It had all different kinds of cool equipment so that all kinds of kids could play on it.

"Yes!" Christina answered. "I go on it every day. The swing is my favorite because I can go really high."

"Oh, I love to swing high," Noelle replied honestly, thinking of the swing in her backyard. It was for little kids, but she still loved to swing on it and just look up at the sky, thinking. "I have a swing in my backyard and it's my favorite too."

"Hey, Christina, Noelle's birthday is today," Noel told her.

"It *is*?" said Christina, her eyes wide. "Right on Christmas? That's so cool. Ours is the night before. Close but not Christmas."

Noelle laughed. She had never thought of it like that

before. "I guess it is pretty special."

"I'm going to skate by myself, okay?" Christina asked Noel. "Watch me!" And she skated away to a woman who was waving to her. Noelle guessed that she must Noel and Christina's mom.

Noel skated up closer to her. "Thanks for being so nice to Christina," he said.

"Why wouldn't I be?" asked Noelle.

"Well, she's different, and sometimes people don't know how to act or what to say," Noel explained. "She just wants everyone to treat her normally. And really she's just like anyone else mostly, except that she does things a little more slowly."

They both watched Christina skate. She glided smoothly on the ice and even did a little twirl.

"I always try to be nice to everybody," Noel said, looking at his sister, "because I always want everyone to be nice to Christina."

So that explains it, Noelle thought. That's how he knew how to speak to Eliza and how he was so patient with James. What a sweet guy. Could he be any nicer?

Then Noelle thought of something. Noel didn't just share his birthday with Christmas Eve, but with a twin.

"So what's it like sharing a birthday?" she asked.

Noel looked a little sheepish. "Honestly?" he said.

"Honestly!" said Noelle.

"Well," began Noel, "you know I love Christina and she gets really excited for our birthday. But just once I'd kind of like to have a birthday by myself, you know? Without celebrating it with Christina. And without Christmas on top of it."

Noelle gave him a sympathetic smile. "You know, I was feeling sorry for myself about having to share my birthday with Christmas, but you have to share your birthday with Christmas *and* a sister. You totally win."

They both laughed.

"Want to skate?" Noel asked.

Noelle grinned. "Let's go!"

They skated around the pond a few times, not saying anything. They stuck together as they dodged the little kids and the slow skaters. On the side of the pond, Noelle spotted her parents. They smiled at her, and her father gave her a really big, corny wave.

Noelle rolled her eyes and replied with a normal little wave. They headed down to the other end of the pond, where Andrew and some of his friends were taking shots with Andrew's hockey stick in the area reserved for hockey.

It was busy and noisy but Noel and Noelle were still quiet as they circled the pond again, as if there was a little bubble around them. After a while, Noel's mother called out.

"Noel! We have to go get ready for Christmas dinner!"

To Noelle's delight, Noel looked a little disappointed at having to leave. She had to restrain herself from doing a little dance.

"Sorry," he said with a shrug.

"It's okay," Noelle replied. "We'll probably be going soon too." They skated toward the benches and sat down on one right under a tree. Noelle looked up and saw that someone had hung a sprig of mistletoe there.

She froze, panicked. Did Noel see it? If so, what would he do? She sat there shivering a little as Noel took off his skates, but not because she was cold.

Noel looked up and saw the mistletoe, breaking into a grin.

"See that?" he said, pointing, and she looked up, trying to pretend she hadn't noticed.

"Um . . . ," she began, but before she could even say

149

anything else, Noel gave her a quick kiss on the cheek.

"It's tradition!" he said, and his face was a little pink. "I hope you have a great birthday, Noelle!" and before she knew it he was hurrying away.

Noelle was so dizzy she could barely speak.

"Merry birthday," she said, and it took her a second to realize that she had mixed up merry Christmas and happy birthday, just like Uncle Marty did.

Noel stopped and gave her a big smile. "That's perfect! Merry birthday, Noelle!"

Noelle sighed happily as she watched him hurry to catch up to Christina and his mom. Then she heard a voice behind her.

"Hey, you're not leaving yet, are you?"

She turned to see Jess, Hailey, and Alyson standing there, holding their skates. Noelle quickly scanned the pond and saw her parents skating in the center of the rink.

"Um, I don't think so," she said.

"So let's skate," Jess said, flopping down beside her and pulling off her boots.

"Are you having a good birthday?" Hailey asked.

Noelle looked around at her friends, who were all

smiling and talking about Christmas. Jess was telling them about the awesome monster Noelle made her. She watched the happy skaters on the pond and the gentle flurries falling down on the scene. Then she touched her cheek. She could still feel a little tingle where Noel had kissed her. She thought about how they skated around, and got a nice warm feeling inside.

Snowflakes were tumbling around, everyone was in a good mood, and she knew she was about ten minutes away from her mom's famous hot chocolate. Even if it wasn't as she had planned, so far her birthday was absolutely perfect.

ANGELA DARLING was nicknamed "The Love Guru" by her friends in school because she always gave such awesome advice on crushes. And Angela's own first crush worked out pretty well . . . they have been married for almost ten years now! When Angela isn't busy watching romantic comedies, reading romance novels, or dreaming up new stories, she works as an editor in New York City. She knows deep down that *every* story can't possibly have a happy ending, but the incurable romantic in her can't help but always look for the silver lining in every cloud.

Here's a sneak peek at the next book in the series:

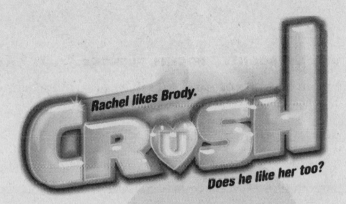

Rachel likes Brody.

Does he like her too?

Rachel's Valentine Crush

"COME ON, ROBBIE," RACHEL PLEADED. "JUST EAT two more bites of broccoli. That's it. Just two more bites."

"Peas, peas, peas," Rachel's little brother sang. "Peas, please. Peas, please."

"We don't have peas tonight," Rachel said for the hundredth time. "We have broccoli. Eat it up so you can have a special treat."

"Peas!" Robbie cried hopefully. He banged his fork on the table.

Rachel leaned toward the sink and turned the water on full blast so that Robbie wouldn't hear her groan.

Bzzzz!

"How's that broccoli coming?" Rachel called out as she dried her hands on her jeans. Then she pulled her cell out of her back pocket. She could already guess that the text was from her best friend, Taylor—even though

Rachel had specifically said that *she* would text Taylor as soon as she was ready. But Taylor wasn't exactly the patient type.

Rach! U ready?

"Peas!" Robbie hollered from the dining room.
"No, broccoli!" Rachel hollered back without looking up from her phone.

No! Still doing dishes and Robbie still eating. Going as fast as I can!!!

But it starts soooooon! Hurry hurry

Believe me, I know

Rachel's phone was already buzzing again as she shoved it back into her pocket, but she decided to ignore it—at least until Robbie finished eating. She suddenly realized that Robbie was quiet. Unusually quiet. Rachel peeked into the dining room, hoping to find his cheeks puffed out with a giant mouthful of broccoli. Instead, she found Robbie grinning at her with a broccoli floret sticking out of each ear.

"Robbie!" Rachel yelled. "You *know* you're not supposed to put food in your ears!"

Robbie's eyes widened.

Then, in a flash, he popped both broccoli bites into his mouth. Rachel blinked in surprise. She'd never seen Robbie eat his most hated food so fast.

"Tweat?" Robbie asked with his mouth full, spraying bits of broccoli onto the table.

"Okay, but chew with your mouth closed," Rachel replied as she ducked back into the kitchen. She stared into the pantry, knowing that her dad didn't like Robbie to eat a lot of sweets. It was the first time that Rachel had been responsible for Robbie's dinner and bedtime all by herself, and she really didn't want to mess it up.

Then again, sometimes Grandma Nellie gave Robbie a treat after dinner. Maybe she would've given him a little dessert tonight if she hadn't been at her Scrapbooking for Seniors meeting. So Rachel plucked three chocolate chips from a half-empty bag and brought them to Robbie.

"Here you go, buddy," she said. "Three chocolate chips for a three-year-old."

Robbie's whole face lit up as he shoved the chocolate chips into his mouth. "My chocolate yums!" he cried. "More, please!"

But Rachel had already whisked his plate off to the dishwasher. She glanced at the clock on the microwave; it read 7:46. She had fourteen minutes to finish the dishes and get Robbie to bed before *The Scoop* came on. Rachel had only watched the gossipy entertainment show once or twice; her dad thought TV shows like that were a giant waste of time. But Rachel hoped that he would make an exception tonight, since she had finished all her homework and her chores before the show started. After all, it wasn't every night that her former classmate, Brody Warner, was interviewed live on national TV!

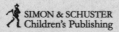